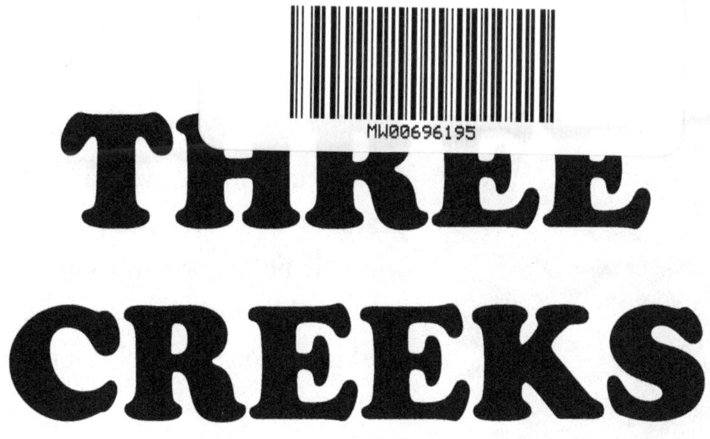

THREE CREEKS

by

KEN FARMER

Cover Art by:
Ken Farmer
Cover model:
Taylor Marie
Photo by Ryan Boring
On behalf of Rising Productions, LLC

: AUTHOR

Ken Farmer didn't write his first full novel until he was sixty-nine years of age. He often wonders what the hell took him so long. At age seventy-nine…he's currently working on novel number thirty-seven.

Ken spent thirty years raising cattle and quarter horses in Texas and forty-five years as a professional actor (after a stint in the Marine Corps). Those years gave him a background for storytelling…or as he has been known to say, "I've always been a bit of a bull---t artist, so writing novels kind of came naturally once it occurred to me I could put my stories down on paper."

Ken's writing style has been likened to a combination of Louis L'Amour and Terry C. Johnston with an occasional Hitchcockian twist…now that's a combination.

In addition to his love for writing fiction, he likes to teach acting, voice-over and writing workshops. His favorite expression is: "Just tell the damn story."

Writing has become Ken's second life: he has been a Marine, played collegiate football, been a Texas wildcatter, cattle and horse rancher, professional film and TV actor and director, and now…a novelist. Who knew?

Ken Farmer's dialogue flows like a beautiful western river…it's the gold standard…Carole Beers

ISBN-13: 978-1-7341765-7-5

Timber Creek Press
Imprint of Timber Creek Productions, LLC
312 N. Commerce St.
Gainesville, Texas 76240

Published by: Timber Creek Press
timbercreekpresss@yahoo.com
www.timbercreekpress.net
Twitter: @pagact
Facebook Book Page:
www.facebook.com/TimberCreekPress
Ken's email: pagact@yahoo.com
214-533-4964

DEDICATION

This tome is dedicated to my grand parents, John L. Franklin Jolley - 1883-1964 and Mary Alice (Mame) Chisholm Jolley - 1885 - 1966 of Union County, Arkansas.

ACKNOWLEDGMENT

The author gratefully acknowledges Lt. Colonel Clyde DeLoach, USMC (Ret.), T.C. Miller, Author, Terry Heflin - retired English Professor at Tarrant County College and Author, award-winning, best-selling author, Mary Deal, best-selling author, Brad Dennison, and Penny (Mom) Tucker for their invaluable help in proofing, beta reading and editing this novel.

FOREWORD

This novel you are about to read is a departure from the usual fiction of Ken Farmer, and yet he tackles it with a familiarity that would make you think he had been writing this type of story for years.

From a literary point of view, you would probably call it a Southern Noir Murder Mystery. And yet it is so much more than that. With this novel, we get a taste of true Americana, a taste of days gone by.

And we get to meet the kind of people who truly built this country, people I believe we need more of today. This novel is so rich in texture you can almost smell the grass and the damp earth underfoot. You can feel the magic of a southern night. Prepare yourself for a ride that you won't soon forget. - Brad Dennison - Author

Three Creeks is a seminal master class.
Robert Joseph Ahola

TIMBER CREEK PRESS

CHAPTER ONE

THREE CREEKS

“No, Daddy, no! I’m scared…” Was all I got out before the waterwings my grandma had made me out of two one gallon lard buckets and a flour sack went sailing into the bushes one way an’ all I could see in the other direction was sky, trees, water, sky, trees, water…

I splashed face first to the surface of the murky creek all the way out in the middle of the swimmin' hole. I came to the surface, spittin' an' sputterin'…tryin' to hold my head above water.

"Put your head down, boy!…Swim to me. Come on…Put your head down…Reach for the bank."

I looked up with water blurin' my vision at my daddy standin' up on the clay bank of the local swimmin' hole at Three Creeks, waving me toward him. He was a hard-as-nails, muscular, square-jawed, broad-shouldered man without a ounce of fat on him.

I was to be eight years old in three days, June 18, 1949…if I survived. My daddy was a driller for Shell Oil and we currently lived just outside of a boomtown named Gainesville, Texas, in some former Army barracks. The base where all the drillin' crews lived had been named Camp Howes durin' the war.

The war they called World War II…guess there'd been another one before…had been over almost four years and we had already lived in seven boomtowns in three states, searchin' for oil during the war an' were still at it. I was born six months before Pearl Harbor.

Daddy tried to enlist in the Army, the Navy, the Marine Corps, an' even the Coast Guard, but they wouldn't let him, said he had a critical occupation, whatever that is...drillin' for oil for the country's war effort.

But, anyway, every summer, we'd go to my mama's home in southern Arkansas just seven miles north of the Louisiana line off the Haynesville Road. That part of the state was known as the deep piney woods.

I could always tell when we were gettin' close. "Daddy, I can smell pine trees."

'Course you have to understand cars weren't air-conditioned in those days, you had to drive with the windows rolled down...Or if it was cold, you cracked the little triangle window in the corner of the front ones, 'specially when mama or daddy were smokin'.

Grandma an' grandpa lived way out in the country on a dirt road in a ramblin' home they referred to as a dog-run house. They called it that on account it had a twelve-foot wide hall down the middle of the house from the big wrap-around front porch to the screened-in porch at the back. There were bedrooms on each side with fireplaces an' grandma's kitchen was at the far end of the house on the other side of the big dinin' room.

There wasn't no electricity or runnin' water. Grandma used coal-oil lamps for light, had a big, wide cast iron woodstove to cook on. I can still remember the taste of her hot buttermilk biscuits with fresh-churned butter an' sorghum syrup in the mornin's.

She counted on us kids to split wood for her wood box beside the stove when we were there an' give grandpa a break.

They had a good deep drilled well that we got to go draw water from with this long, skinny galvanized well bucket. There was a two-holer outhouse about sixty feet from the back door.

Grandpa was born in 1883 and had retired from the sheriff's department at the end of the war. He was now a truck farmer—everbody called him Big John…Big John Jamison. He was about 6'3" an' weighed around 285…Nobody messed with Big John. He wore blue bib overalls ever day over his longhandle top with the sleeves cut off in the summertime.

Us grand kids had been told he once picked up a bale of cotton on his back and carried it thirty feet on a bet. Believe a bale a cotton weighs about five hundred pounds or maybe more. Don't know if that's true or not, but we all believed it.

For such a big man, he was gentle with us kids...was actually afraid to spank us. He'd leave any discipline that had to be dealt out to grandma.

Her name was Mame...well, it was Mary Alice, but he always called her Mame an' she couldn't of weighed a hundred pounds soakin' wet. She would be the one to tear our butts up when we needed it, usually with a peach tree switch we'd have to go cut ourselves.

We'd go to their house when school was out for daddy's vacation cause he liked to go fishin' with mama's brothers an' their kids—our cousins. She had one sister an' four brothers an' there was a real passel of first, second an' third cousins lived fair close.

One brother, Uncle J.B., his wife, Aunt Thelma an' my three cousins, Jessie, Don, an' Hubbert, lived about a hundred yards down a sandy road from grandma an' grandpa. The others lived eighteen miles away in El Dorado, Arkansas.

Mama's sister, Aunt Anna Lee, an' her husband Uncle Ford, lived near Homer, Louisiana with their four kids.

Daddy an' mama would leave my older brother an' me there for the summer when his two weeks was up an' he had to go back to work—we lived for the summer. Never had to wear shoes, 'ceptin' on Sunday for church.

Like I said, grandma had made me this set of waterwings, on account I couldn't swim yet, for when we'd go down to Three Creeks. It was about two miles from the house by road.

It was a fairly large area because three creeks came together an' that's where everybody around came to swim…most of them were relatives of some sort. It was also used for baptisms an' was surrounded by big trees an' grapevines an' grandpa had hung a rope swing from one of the oaks that hung out over the water. He would go down there to take a bath…even in the winter.

I think daddy finally got tired of puttin those cans in that flour sack an' figured it was high time I learned how to swim…

"Kick your feet, Sunshine! Pull the water to you. Come on…come to me…Kick…Kick."

Don't know if I was more scared of drownin' or of him, but I did what he said—put my head down, kicked my feet and pulled the water to me.

"Good job, Foot!"

I had been christened Henry Lightfoot Lee after a couple of ancestors on my daddy's side of the Lee family of Virginia. They said Henry 'Lighthorse Harry' Lee was a hero of the American Revolution an' Francis Lightfoot Lee was one of the signers of the Declaration of Independence.

Somehow between when I was born an' now my name got shortened to just 'Foot'...Oh, an' Lighthorse Harry was Robert E. Lee's daddy.

I looked up, rubbed the water out of my eyes as he leaned over, grabbed my arm and pulled me up—I made it, but I screamed bloody murder while I was still in the air.

"Hurt you, boy?" He set me down on the bank.

"Daddy, Daddy, I stepped on somebody just 'fore you pulled me out."

He knelt down in front of me, glanced over at the murky water then back at me. "What are you talkin' 'bout, Foot?...There's nobody in there."

"Yes, there was...Honest Injun, Daddy, I stepped on somebody."

He studied my face for a minute, got to his feet an' dove headfirst into the creek…He was wearin' some cut-off jeans for a bathin' suit just like I was.

My brother, Bobby, an' cousins…Don an' Hubert, ran up to where I was to watch Daddy as he swam back to the bank an' commenced to feel around with his foot.

Then of a sudden, he dove under the water an' in a couple of seconds he come back to the surface an' had a blonde-headed young girl in his arms.

Her name was Bethany Cade…she was fifteen or thereabouts…everbody knew who she was. There was thirteen or so in the Cade family…nobody knew for sure…an' they all lived in this one shotgun shack over near Jolley's Store. My cousins said they was inbred…whatever that means.

Bethany's head flopped over to the side, with her blonde hair hangin' limply as Daddy waded out of the water with her in his arms…could tell right off she was dead…

Daddy laid her on the top of the bank, turned an' ran to our '39 Ford sedan up on the road, got a towel, brought it back an' covered her face.

"Now you boys stay here, I'm gonna go get your grandpa, he'll know who to contact…an' don't touch her, hear?"

We all nodded as he ran back up to the loggin' road that went past the swimmin' hole, started ol' Huldy, turned her around an' drove off in a cloud of dust.

Cousin Hubert, he was a year younger'n me asked, "What'd she feel like, Foot?"

I shrugged my shoulders. "Kinda mushy an' slick."

He reached his foot toward Bethany's arm.

"Hubert! You heard Uncle Joe."

Don pushed him away from her body. He was about the same age as my brother, Bobby, three years older'n me.

Daddy's name was really Bob, or Robert, but the family all called him Joe, don't know why…happened 'fore I come along.

The sun was settlin' down toward the tops of the trees 'round Three Creeks.

Hubert looked up. "Hope Uncle Joe gets back here with grampaw 'fore it gits dark."

Bobby looked over at him. "Why, what's the big deal?"

"Just don't want to be down here in the bottom with no dead body's all."

Don turned from starin' down at Bethany. "How come? She's dead."

"Yeah but Mamie…"

Mamie was grandma's colored washer woman who was born on the place an' said her grandma and grandpa was slaves for my great great grandpa, but none of 'em would leave when he freed 'em durin' Lincoln's war…Mamie said they was manumitted, whatever that means. Great great grandpa let 'em all be sharecroppers so's they could make a livin'.

"Well, Mamie says haints come out when it turns dark where somebody's just died…'specially down in the bottoms." Hubert turned an' looked around at the darkening deep woods on all sides of the creek.

Don suddenly grabbed his arm an' yelled, "Boo!"

Hubert nearly jumped out of his skin, turned and whaled on his older brother with both fists. "Dang, you! Don't do that. Ain't fair…I'm gonna tell mama."

Don bent over laughin'. "Shoulda told Uncle Joe to bring back a sugar tit while he was gitttin' grampa."

"You just wait."

We heard the brakes squeal on daddy's Ford up to the road an' in a minute him and grandpa were comin' down the slope through the woods.

Grandpa walked right up to Bethany's body, knelt down an' pulled the towel off. He studied her for a few minutes, turned her head to the right then the left an' looked up at daddy.

"Been strangled, Joe. See the bruise marks around her neck?"

Daddy leaned over an' looked where he was pointin'. "Can even see the thumb prints on the front."

"Uh-huh…Used both hands. Strong man…broke her neck. Heard the bones grind when I turned her head."

§§§

CHAPTER TWO

THREE CREEKS

"If you'll stay with the body an' keep the varmints away, I'd appreciate it, Joe…An' you don't mind, I'll borrow your car, go to Jolley's Store, call the coroner's office an' the Sheriff an' give 'em a report…Take 'em thirty, forty-five minutes to get out here from town."

"Why don't you take the boys on home while you're at it, John…'Magine Mame has supper 'bout ready."

"Can I stay with you, Daddy?"

"Naw, Foot, you need to get on to the house…You're already cold. Your lips 'er blue an' I can see you shakin'."

"I'll be awright…'sides, you might need some help."

Daddy tried to hide a grin. "Well, if I do, Hossfly, guess I'll muddle through somehow…Now, you go on with your grandpa an' Bobby, Don, an' Hubert. Tell your mama I'll be home directly…Keep some supper warm."

I looked down at my bare feet with my toes diggin' in the dirt on the creek bank—arguin' with daddy was like tryin' to pee up a rope. "Yessir." 'Sides it was gittin' dark.

Grandpa headed up the path toward the road, Bobby, Don, an' Hubert had already run ahead of him to the car. I heard Don call shotgun.

I looked at Bethany again. Her thin cotton dress that didn't cover much was made out of those colored flour sacks with patterns on 'em an' was startin' to dry in the late afternoon heat. Then I looked back to daddy. He was just standin' there, his arms folded cross his chest, an' starin' at the water in the creek. I turned an' ran through the darkenin' shadows after the others.

'Bout halfway up the path, I stepped on somethin' round an' softer than a stick. I musta jumped 'bout four feet in the air, let out a yelp an' turned on the speed. Knew in my heart it was a moccasin, but wadn't 'bout to stop to turn around an' see what kind...just ran like my hair was on fire. Been chased by cottonmouths 'fore...They're mean as sin...'specially when you pester 'em.

Jolley's Store was 'bout two miles from Three Creeks an' was the only place around you could buy anythin' you might need without drivin' all the way into El Dorado. It was kinda what you might call a general store—had one of most everthing.

The owner was Smead Jolley. Grandpa said he was some kinda cousin...'course purtnear everybody in this part of Arkansas seemed to be cousins or close to it...heard he had played baseball for the Chicago White Sox.

THREE CREEKS

The store had been there on the Haynesville Road long as I could remember, which wasn't no real great shakes on account of I was only eight…well, in three days.

Cousin Smead would say when you come in the door, "If I ain't got it, you don't need it."

The lights out under the porch were off when grandpa pulled up an' stopped. Don had got the front seat with Bobby, Hubert, an' me the back. I sat behind grandpa. I could see a light in the rear of the store—cousin Smead had already closed for the night, I guess, an' must of been in the back countin' his money.

Grandpa climbed the four steps of the stoop to the porch, stepped over old Blue, cousin Smead's coon dog, who wasn't 'bout to move for wood, water or coal, and banged on the side of the screen door with his ham-like fist.

It had one of those metal signs across the front that said *MEADS FINE BREAD* across it—must of been there holdin' the door together 'cause it looked kinda flimsy.

There was a big metal coke ice box with *NEHI* painted on the front next to the door—had a big padlock on the lid so's nobody could steal a soda pop durin' the night.

"Smead! Smead! It's John. Need to use the telephone."

He banged a couple more times…thought the door was gonna fall off.

"Smead!"

"Comin', I'm comin'. Keep yer shirt on, Big John…Good goshamighty, tear my door up."

He unlocked the wood door that had glass on the top, then unhooked the screen door so's grandpa could open it. Smead an' grandpa was 'bout same age…guess they grew up together.

"Now, what's all this about, John?"

"Found a body down to Three Creeks…one of the Cade gals. Looked like somebody strangled an' then threw her in the creek. Gotta call Sheriff Wilson an' the coroner to come out."

I could hear him tellin' cousin Smead all this through the open doorway while he strode toward the telephone on the wall behind the counter with the cash register.

"Naw! Really?…Which one of 'em was it?"

Grandpa cranked the handle on the side. "Looked to be Bethany, to me…Mabel, this is Big

John Jamison, get me the sheriff…No, I mean right now."

"Oh, Lordy, she was Clara's favorite. Gonna kill her."

"Sheriff?…Yeah, this is John. Got a body out to Three Creeks…murdered…Tell you who when you and Ralph get out here. Meet you at Three Creeks…Awright." The receiver made a click when he hung it up.

Smead looked at grandpa when he turned around. "How's come you didn't tell him who it was?"

Grandpa pulled off his battered old fedora and wiped the band inside with his handkerchief an' looked at Smead from under his brows.

"You know anythin' said over that telephone of yours, Mabel will have it over the whole damn county by mornin'."

"Oh, right, didn't think about that…Guess you want me to keep quiet 'bout all this then?"

"Purty close, Smead. 'Preciate the use of your telephone. Got some of the grand kids out in Joe's car. Best get 'em to the house 'fore I head back out to the swimin' hole."

"'Nytime. You know that, John."

Not sure grandpa heard him ‘cause he was already out the door an’ down the stoop. He opened the door, got in, an’ pushed the starter button on the floorboard to crank ‘er up.

Grandma an’ grandpa‘s house was behind Jolley’s store three or four hundred yards on a side dirt road that us grand kids all called the red hill where it turned to the south after it passed their house.

We used to play on it when it rained. Really would make Mamie mad ‘cause she had to boil our muddy clothes twice in her cast iron wash pot out back of the house.

He pulled up and stopped under some big old sycamore trees that was across the front of the yard. We all piled out and ran up the rock sidewalk to the front porch. Grandma an’ mama were sittin’ in slat-backed, calf-hide bottom rockers waitin’.

My dog, Tiny, a red and white fox terrier an’ whippet cross was at her feet. She jumped up when we ran up the steps an’ danced ‘round my bare feet.

“You boys all right?”

Grandma got up from the rocker. Could tell she’d been dippin’ snuff on account there was always somethin’ a little dark in one of the tiny wrinkles at the corner of her mouth. She didn't want anybody to know she dipped an' always carried one of those small cans of Garrett Snuff a little bigger'n a spool of thread in her dress pocket…but we did anyway.

She gave me a big hug after grandpa told her what happened. "That was so awful, you findin' pore Bethany like that…she was such a sweet child…considerin'."

"Uh-huh." I leaned back from her.

"Bet ya'll are 'bout hungry, aren'tcha?"

We all answered with a quick, 'Yessum,' as Grandpa climbed the steps up to the porch.

"Need my flashlight, Mame…you or Vertis get it for me? My shoes are dirty, don't want to mess up your floor…Oh, an' a coal oil lantern."

Vertis was my mama, well, her full name was Johnie Vertis, she was named after grandpa, but all the family called her Vertis, don't know why. I always called her Mama, of course.

Grandma went to get his flashlight 'cause she knew where it was, brought it an' the lamp out an' handed them to him.

"We'll have to go over to the Cades tomorrow with some food. Know Clara's goin' to be beside herself, besides, she's carryin' another one, you know."

Grandpa shook his head. "Nope, didn't know. Hard to keep track the way she churns 'em out."

"John L.!"

He ducked his head. "Well, it's the truth."

"Don't have to say everything you know, John L. Franklin Jamison."

"Yessum."

Think she was the only thing in this world grandpa was scared of.

THREE CREEKS

The three-quarter gibbous moon had risen above the trees down at the swimming hole casting flickering gold and silver flashes of light like sparkling diamonds on the surface of the slow moving water.

Joe sat down on the bank next to Bethany's body with his arms wrapped around his knees waiting on the sheriff, coroner, and Big John. He had pulled the towel back over her face.

The night creatures, frogs, crickets, locust, and birds had started up their symphony of sounds. A rain crow in a close-by tree made his unusual call. *Cherk...cherk...cherk...cherk-cher-cher-cher-cher.* To tell all who listened there was rain coming in a day or so.

The creek didn't make any noise, though, as it flowed slowly toward the Ouachita River and eventually the Gulf of Mexico.

Occasionally the sound of a fish's tail slapping the water would add to the other sounds as serenity reclaimed the bottom.

A louder than normal 'whoosh' of water from the creek brought his head up to study the pool in front of him. *Musta been an alligator gar. John says there's some big ones in here an' some snappin' turtles big as a number three washtub.*

The 'whoosh' came again, from upstream a little above the swimming hole.

Joe got to his feet and studied the water where flowed out of the canopied creek into the moonlight toward him.

"What the…Oh, damn."

§§§

CHAPTER THREE

UNION COUNTY, ARKANSAS

Sheriff Myron Wilson drove his county vehicle, a 1948 black Ford sedan south on the Haynesville Road—balding, skinny as a rail County Coroner, Ralph Duckworth sat in the passenger seat next to him.

Doctor Duckworth peered through his side of the windshield at the oil-topped black road in front of them, which soaked up the light from the Ford's headlamps like a sponge. "Glad that moon's up, wouldn't be able to see doodle-squat if it wasn't."

"One of these days they'll be makin' headlamps that light far enough out to keep from runnin' over some farmer's cow…now that the war's over."

"I'd say…If they can make one of those atomic bomb things like they did, I 'spect they can make most anything…Might even make somethin' that'll get man to the moon."

"Don't get carried away, there, Doc. Flash Gordon an' Buck Rogers are just comic strips."

"Just sayin' is all." Doctor Duckworth looked out the open side window at the dark trees slipping by at the Sheriff's modest forty miles per hour speed. "What kind of body you think Big John's got?"

"A dead one, I 'magine."

"Dammit, you know what I mean, Myron."

The sheriff glanced over at the sixty year old physician and county medical examiner. "Don't know. Just hope it ain't another young girl is all…'Cause a panic if it is."

"Oh, surely not…Maybe it's just somebody that went swimmin' an' drowned."

"Big John said murdered...Wore a badge long enough to know the difference."

The doctor nodded. "Yep, never known Big John to be wrong."

"Too bad he turned his badge in an' went back to farmin'."

Sheriff Wilson pursed his lips. "Just hope I can get him to pin it back on...leastwise for this case if it turns out to be another murdered young girl."

"Did he say anythin' 'bout how the person died?...Strangled or what?"

The somewhat portly long time sheriff shook his head as he pulled off the main road to the logging trail that ran down to the swimming hole. "Let's hope not."

THREE CREEKS

Big John looked through the trees at the glow approaching from the direction of the main road. "Looks like the sheriff an' Ralph finally made it."

Joe got to his feet from where he was squatting and looked through the trees also. "Yeah, 'spect he's goin' to be a mite upset when he gets here."

"Both of 'em will."

The lights through the trees went out, followed by the double thunks of car doors closing up on the logging road.

John had lit and set the coal oil lantern on the ground at the head of two bodies lying side by side on the bank of the creek.

Two small pale yellow flashlight beams dancing around through the brush showed from up the trail, then they entered the bare area beside the swimming hole.

"Sheriff…Doc. Made decent time."

"Did, John…Whatchu got?…Oh, good God."

Both flashlight beams panned over the two bodies, each with towels over their faces.

"This here's my son-in-law, Joe Lee, in from Texas…Joe, Sheriff Wilson an' Doctor Duckworth…"

The three men exchanged quick handshakes.

"…Joe found both bodies, well, actually my grandson, Foot, found the first, Bethany Cade…an' Joe pulled the second out while I was gone callin' ya'll…Looks like Loretta Harker."

Doctor Duckworth knelt down and examined both girls, especially their necks. "Strangled an' both with broken necks." He looked up. "Each one's 'bout fifteen…I'God, Myron, we got us a Jim Cracker, mother lovin' chain killer."

"Think they've been violated?"

He shook his head. "Won't know 'bout that till I get 'em on my table…The Harker girl was killed last, though."

Sheriff Wilson bent over and put his hands on his knees still a bit winded from the jaunt through the woods. "How can you tell?"

He placed his hand on Loretta's flat stomach. "Still got a little body heat left…Bethany don't. She's showin' rigor in her jaw an' neck which would be at two to six hours…but the temperature of the water an' how long she's been in it would have an' effect."

"How do you know all that stuff, Doc?"

He looked at the sheriff over the top of his wire-rimmed glasses. "One, I'm a doctor, Myron, an' two…I read a lot of Sherlock Holmes an' Hercule Poirot." Ralph looked back down at the bodies, a slight impish grin played across his face.

"Huh?"

"Just trust me, Myron."

"You gonna put 'em in that new county sedan, Sheriff?"

Wilson glanced over at Big John. "Not on your life. Called the hospital to bring out an am'lance from the morgue 'fore we left. Should be here most anytime." He turned to Joe. "Where'd Foot find Bethany, Mister Lee?"

"Mister Lee was my daddy, Sheriff...He stepped on her underwater at the edge of the bank here."

Joe walked over to the creek and pointed. The bank didn't slope into the creek, but dropped straight down.

"Hadn't been in the water long enough to gas up an' float again, Myron." The coroner moved over to the edge. "Say less than two hours...my guess."

"The other body floated in from upstream, Joe?"

"Yep, was bein' bumped along by alligator gar or maybe snappin' turtles...What made me notice it in the dark, Sheriff."

Myron looked off to the upstream side of the hole. "Need to canvas out the area tomorrow when there's light...You give me a hand, John?"

"Got roastin' ears need pullin' tomorrow, Sheriff. You know...or lose 'em."

"Can probably take care of that with the boys, John. Shouldn't be any hill for a stepper...Done it many's the time for my daddy growin' up in Navarro County back in Texas."

John nodded. "Have to deliver 'em to my route customers in El Dorado on Saturday...'long with the tomatoes an' squash that has to be gathered tomorrow, probably the okra, too...Busy season."

"Can handle it. Don't have to be back to work for a little over another week yet."

"Hate to give you my problems on your vacation, Joe."

He chuckled. "No problem, John, a little work...but no problem."

"Know you were lookin' forward to goin' fishin' over to the Ouachita with J.B. an' them."

"We'll get it in...later. First things first." He looked down at the bodies. "These little girls need some justice."

JAMISON HOME

Me, Bobby, Don, an' Hubert finished up our supper of purple hull crowder peas, hot water cornbread, fried okra, an' pan steak, with ice tea in Mason jars…

Grandma an' mama come in from the kitchen with four bowls of steamin' dewberry cobbler.

"Don't suppose ya'll want any of this…was fixin't to throw it to the hogs."

We all nearly jumped up off the bench we were sittin' on that ran the whole length of the big dinin' table. There were chairs on the other side for the grownups an' at each end for grandma an' grandpa. His was extra big with arms on it on account of…well, on account he was grandpa.

The grand kids all had to sit on the bench with any little ones at the round breakfast table in the kitchen.

"Oh, golly whiz, Grandma don't do that." I looked at my brother an' cousins. "We saved some room on account we smelled your cobbler when we come in from the porch…ain't that right, ya'll?"

Don, bein' the oldest, nodded. "Oh, yessum, sure wouldn't want to see it go to the hogs."

"'Sides, Grandpa said we're gonna have to help pull roastin' ears an' gather the maters an' squash, an' probably the cucumbers tomorrow…early 'fore it gets hot," commented Bobby. "He said we were gonna need a good supper."

I held up my hand. "Daddy said to keep his warm, too."

"Already got his an your granddaddy's in the warmin' oven…Sure they'll be ready to eat, time they get home."

It always amazed me how grandma could look so fresh, when that wood cook stove sure put out some heat…'specially in the summertime.

Mama said that since all the rooms in grandma's house had twelve foot ceilin's, that's where the heat went, an' then them things above the doorways called transoms let the breeze carry it away an' out the screened-in back porch. That's a pretty slick idea, ask me…Think she closes 'em come wintertime, though.

THREE CREEKS

Sheriff Wilson looked up the slope toward the road at the lights from a vehicle that turned and pointed down at the creek. Then they shown back the other way as the driver turned the unit around.

"Am'lance. Hope they don't have to make two trips."

The two attendants came down the trail with a litter between them. Both men had been combat medic veterans in the war—had seen most everything.

"Gonna need another litter, Pete," said Doctor Duckworth when the men entered the clearing.

The medic at the front, Pete, glanced at the two bodies in the dim light from the lantern. "Oh, Jesus Christ an' all his disciples, Doc…They're just teens…"

They set the stretcher on the ground, loaded Bethany Cade on it and trudged back up the trail to the ambulance. In a short moment, they were back for Loretta Harker.

"Didn't know there were two, Doc."

"We didn't either till we got here, Pete."

"Know the Harker's…Good people. Just never seen this comin'…This makes four now, don't it, Doc?"

He nodded, puffed out his cheeks and exhaled loudly. "That we know about."

"Good thing the hospital got those Army surplus ambulances, plenty room."

They all turned an looked up toward the road at what appeared to be two more sets of headlights coming down the logging road.

The sheriff shook his head. “Oh, Lordy, Lordy.”

§§§

CHAPTER FOUR

THREE CREEKS

Sheriff Wilson turned to Pete and Charlie, the other medic. “Ya’ll get your asses outta here. Be damn sure you keep her covered…an’ don’t talk to the sons-a-bitches. Hear? Don’t want the bastards bollixin’ things up.”

“Didn’t have to tell us, Sheriff. Didn’t fall off’n Big John’s watermelon truck, you know.”

The two medics disappeared up the trail before the sheriff could reply.

The Sheriff, Doctor Duckworth, Big John, and Joe Lee heard the double back doors of the Army surplus ambulance close with bangs just before multiple voices began trying to ask the medics questions. The words weren't clear, but they didn't have to be.

The ambulance roared to life, lights came on, and then disappeared back up the logging trail to the main road where they turned north toward El Dorado and the glow vanished.

The sheriff looked at the doctor, held up a hand and folded his fingers one at a time. "Five…four…thre…"

"Sheriff, Sheriff, how many bodies did the ambulance take to town?"

The reporter from the El Dorado News-Times strode into the clearing and got right in his face with a small spiral bound notebook in one hand and a stub of a yellow #2 pencil in the other.

A brown well-creased fedora was pushed to the back of his head and an unlit Lucky Strike cigarette hung from the side of his mouth—it bobbed up and down as he talked.

The entire swimming hole area lit up like it was daylight briefly as his shooter grabbed a picture of the reporter talking to Sheriff Wilson with Doctor Duckworth in the background.

The photographer popped the spent flashbulb out of the attached flash reflector of his Graflex Speed Graphic press camera, put it in the side pocket of his wrinkled sport coat, took a fresh one out, licked the base, and twisted it into the socket.

"Now, dammit, Maybrook, you know I can't tell you that."

"Was there more than one?"

"What'd I just say?"

The news reporter from the local radio station muscled his way next to Clarence Maybrook with a similar notebook. "Sheriff…Murf Smith, KFTW radio…Was it young girls again?"

"Said all I'm gonna say, Murf. No information goes out till the next of kin is notified."

"So you're sayin' there's been another murder?" stated Maybrook.

"Didn't say no such a blamed thing." He turned to Duckworth. "Did I, Ralph?"

The coroner shook his head. "Not that I heard."

Smith turned and looked at Joe. "Is this man a suspect? Never seen him before."

Joe's neck kind of flared as he took a step toward the radio reporter. Big John held out a massive arm to block him, then turned to Smith.

"Murf, suggest you turn around and scuttle back to your car while you still can before my son-in-law tears your head off and craps in your chest cavity…Now, I'd do it before I drop my arm."

Even in the pale light from the lantern on the ground, it was obvious the reporter blanched as he backed up several steps.

The area lit up again, temporarily blinding everyone as the shooter took another picture, this time of Big John and Joe.

Sheriff Wilson calmly took off his gray Stetson, looked at the sweatband, then up at the two reporters and the photographer. "Now, boys, I'm just about a frog's hair from losin' my temper." He glanced at John and Joe. "And these two men are closer than that…It won't be a pretty sight, I guarandamntee you…Now, my office will release a statement when I'm damn good and ready…Not goin' to say this again…Get your scrawny asses out of my sight…" his voice tailed off to a barely audible hiss as he rested the heel of his right hand on the grip of his Colt .38 Police Special revolver at his hip.

The three news hounds started backing away from the piercing brown eyes of the intimidating long time county sheriff.

The creek bottom illuminated once more as the photographer took a quick picture of the four men glaring back with Sheriff Wilson pretty much in the center. Then they all turned and hustled up the path to their vehicles.

Doctor Duckworth had a wry smile on his face. “Think they’ve been watchin’ too many Spencer Tracy newspaper movies.”

The sheriff glanced at his friend. “You think?”

JAMISON HOME

Grandma looked over at Don an’ Hubert sittin’ with me an’ Bobby on the stoop where we were countin’ fireflies out in the yard.

“Don, you an’ Hubert better head on down to the house. Your mama will be wonderin’ ‘bout you.”

He looked off to his right at the lights of their house just a hundred yards down a sandy road from grandma‘s. It was never graded or anythin’, just made by grandpa‘s truck an’ Uncle JB’s car. There was a grass strip in the middle.

“Yessum.” He got to his feet. “Come on, Hubert.”

“Ya’ll want a lamp?”

“Aw, no ma’am. Can get to the house with our eyes closed. Ain’t that right, Hubert?”

“Uh-huh.”

Bobby glanced at our cousins. “Don’t ya’ll step on no snakes on the way…They like to lay in the warm sand after the sun goes down…I hear.”

We were all still in our cutoff jeans an’ barefoot, which is the way we usually ran around all day anyhow.

Hubert looked at his brother, then at grandma. “Well, maybe we ought to take one…so’s we don’t step in any of them goathead patches in the middle of the road…or nothin’.”

Grandma grinned, got out of her rocker an’ went inside. In a minute she came back out with a coal oil lantern, already lit, an’ handed it to Don.

"I'll bring it back when we come in the mornin' for the pickin'."

"Be fine, I'll be sure to have plenty of hot biscuits an' sausage gravy for breakfast…in case ya'll want'ny."

Don an' Hubert exchanged quick glances an' grins.

They waved bye as they headed down the walk to the road out front of the house that led down to theirs. Don carried the lantern.

I laughed an' looked at Bobby. "See the look on their faces when grandma mentioned biscuits an' sausage gravy?"

He nodded an' glanced at grandma as she sat back down in her rocker. "Aunt Thelma can't do gravy worth a flip…got more lumps in it than I got marbles in my sack."

"Now, you watch your mouth, John Robert."

He grinned an' ducked his head. "Yessum…but it's true."

"Bless her heart, she tries."

"Jessie's a better cook than Aunt Thelma." Jessie was Don an' Hubert's older sister. She's fourteen. Got the sweets on a local fella, Leo Ware, he's seventeen. He's really a neat guy.

"She is. Jessie's been helpin' me cook Sunday dinners since she was 'bout nine."

Sunday dinner was always somethin' else at grandma's. She'd have two or three meats, like fried chicken, a ham, an' a roast. There'd be yeast rolls an' cornbread, 'long with field peas, mashed potatoes an' gravy, an' maybe fried squash or okra, an' fresh sliced tomatoes—then a pie or two or cobbler. We'd eat on left overs for a couple days.

Mama smiled at grandma. "Nobody cooks better than you, Mama."

"Oh, pshaw." She got to her feet again. "You boys like some hot milk?"

"Oh, wow! Yessum, if you please."

Grandma went through the screen door, lettin' it close behind her with a bang. Bobby an' me exchanged excited glances. She made her hot milk with fresh sweet milk, some sugar an' a bit of vanilla flavorin'…Tasted kinda like melted ice cream. I like it better'n hot chocolate.

In a minute, she came back out on the front porch with two steamin' mugs an' handed 'em to us.

"Thank you, Grandma."

Mama sniffed the smell, looked at grandma an' got up. "Think I'll go in an' make me a cup, Mama."

She grinned. "Made enough for us too, Vertis."

"You always know what to do, Mama...I'll bring 'em out. You sit down."

Mama got up an' went inside. Just as the screen door slammed shut, grandma turned and looked over her shoulder. "Best bring four cups on a tray. See John an' Joe pullin' in off the road up yonder...You know they'll want some."

"Yes, Mama."

Daddy's Ford pulled up under the sycamore trees out front an' him an' grandpa got out an' walked up to the house. Daddy still had his cutoff jeans on, but they were dry now. He'd pulled a white under shirt on since we'd left Three Creeks.

Grandpa carried the coal oil lantern with him an' his flashlight.

"Ya'll sit down, John. Vertis is bringin' a couple of cups of my hot milk. Figured you might want some when you smelled the boys drinkin' it. Supper's in the warmin' oven when you finish."

"Sounds good, Mame. Been a stressful evenin', what with Joe findin' another body down to the creek 'fore I got back."

Grandma set up. "What?" Who?"

"Little Loretta Harker."

"Oh, no! Where was she?"

Grandpa glanced to daddy.

"Saw her floatin' in the creek on the current, Mame. Gars an' turtles were worryin' her body…Not sure where she came from…"

"I'm helpin' Myron in the mornin' check the area up an' downstream. Joe's gonna handle the pullin' an' pickin' with the boys for me."

"Oh, land sakes! Was she…"

Grandpa nodded. "She was strangled too."

"My, my. What's the world comin' to?"

"Doc Duckworth an' the medic boys from the hospital got 'em loaded in the ambulance 'fore the newspaper an' the radio newshawks got there."

"How'd they know?…Never mind. Mabel an' that party line of Smead's I guess."

Mama came out the screen door with the tray an' four cups of hot milk.

She extended the tray first to grandma, then to daddy an' grandpa. They took their cups an' sat down in the other rockers. Mama got hers, put the tray on the porch an' sat down too.

Grandma looked at mama. "We got quite a bit of cookin' to do in the mornin', Vertis. Joe pulled another body from the creek 'fore John got back…the Harper girl."

"Oh, Mama, no! She was so little last time I saw her last year at the revival meeting when we were here."

"The sheriff's gonna pick me up in the mornin' so Joe can have the truck to load the corn an' things on." He looked at daddy. "Alright they use your car to run the food over to the Cade's an' the Harker's?"

"Sure, John, you know that. They'll have to wait till the Doc notifies the families first, don't you think?"

"Oh, damnation, nearly forgot." Grandpa nodded. "He'll go by an' pick up that Tabernacle of God preacher, Matthew Martin, to go with him in the mornin'. Both families are part of his flock."

Tabernacle of God was what everbody called a Pentecostal church, some folks say Bible thumpers or holy rollers, not real sure why.

Daddy shook his head. “Now there’s a real contradiction.”

Grandpa took a sip of his hot milk and glanced at daddy. “How so?”

“A man of God an’ looks for all the world like a used car salesman…A little too slick for my tastes.”

Mama’s blue eyes kinda snapped. “Robert Reese, that’s a terrible thing to say.”

Daddy just shrugged, glanced at me an’ Bobby an’ winked.

§§§

CHAPTER FIVE

JAMISON HOME

The big red rooster let the world know how special he was as the sky was turning gray to the east an' the beginnin's of golden arrows were just showin' above the trees. Grandpa always said that he thinks he's takin' credit for the sun comin' up.

Me an' Bobby slept in a feather bed, with our dog, Tiny, next to grandma an' grandpa's room so there wasn't no sleepin' in when they got up. Grandma was always first outta bed, 'cause she had to get the fire started in the cook stove so she could fix breakfast an' the coffee.

Her hair was snow white, some folks would say purtnear silver, an' reached to her waist. She'd take it down, give it one hundred strokes with her hoghair brush, an' then put it in one thick braid in the middle for the night. In the mornin' she'd undo it an' put it up in a bun on the back of her head so's she could work.

I couldn't believe it first time I saw her pin all that hair in a knot the size of a baseball—an' do it in less than three minutes. She said it was just practice.

It was easy to hear grandpa—all 285 pounds of him—walk down the big wide hallway with his ankle boots in his hand. He called 'em Thomas Jefferson brogans—don't know why 'cause they didn't look that old.

He also took their parlor pot with him so's he could dump it down the outhouse after he put his boots on an' 'fore he went to the barn to milk Sally.

Time he finished, grandma would have the coffee ready an' the biscuits in the oven.

All the times I spent at their house, grandpa always whistled the same tune while he walked down that long dog run to the front door to put his brogan boots on sittin' on the stoop. I never heard it anywhere else, think it was somethin' he made up—it was catchy though. I sometimes whistle it myself.

Me an' Bobby was sittin' at the breakfast table in the kitchen with daddy. Mama was helpin' grandma with the rest of breakfast. She poured daddy a big white mug of coffee. He liked it plain old black on account that's the way they drank it out on the rig—an' me an' Bobby wanted buttermilk.

Don an' Hubert came in the kitchen. Both looked like they were still asleep, but they made it to the table without runnin' into anything—don't know how they made it from their house. Mama poured them some buttermilk too.

Grandma took out the first pan of biscuits from the oven. She always made them in what she called a flop-over skillet, think it's also called a omelet pan. They were just perfect on both sides—awesome for biscuits an' gravy an' most anythin' else for that matter.

She dumped 'em in a plate on the table an' put some more dough in the pan for another batch. We'd go through at least three pans of biscuits ever mornin'—loved grandma's biscuits. We all just helped ourselves.

Grandpa came in the kitchen with the near full milk bucket an' set it on the counter. "Fix me five, six eggs, Mame, an' a couple rashers of bacon. Gonna be a long day, I'm afraid."

He was wearin' his usual blue bib overalls an' shirt with the sleeves cut off. Saw a lump in his back right pocket an' could tell right off it was his handgun.

He was given a Colt semiautomatic…called it a 1911 or somethin' like that, by Tom Rayford. He was a veteran of that big war they said was World War I who took care of Jolley's Chapel Cemetery just down the road—dug graves an' such.

Mister Tom lived in a little concrete house they let him build right there next to the cemetery on a acre of ground. He surrounded the house with a bunch of orchard trees…apples, peaches, pears, plum, an' figs.

Grandpa said he was a Marine an' fought the Germans in some place overseas call Belleau Wood…musta been a kind of forest or somethin'. The Germans called the Marines 'Devil Dogs'…I wanna be a Marine when I grow up.

Mama filled grandpa's cup an' set it on the table next to a saucer. He poured some in it, picked it up, blew across the top an' then took a sip—called it 'saucered an' blowed'.

There was a knock at the back screen door.

"Come on in, Myron." Grandma saw the sheriff standin' on the back stoop through the kitchen door to the dog run.

He opened the screen door an' took his hat off as he stepped inside.

"Wash up if you want breakfast, Myron. Hang your hat on one of those hooks."

"Yessum."

The sheriff hung his hat like he was told, grabbed a bar of Lifebuoy soap an' poured a couple of dippers in the pan on the washin' shelf from the bucket that hung above it. He soaped up his hands, rinsed them in the pan, an' then dried 'em on the towel hangin' from a hook beside the shelf.

He grabbed a chair after steppin' into the kitchen an' sat down as mama filled a coffee cup for him—he liked it black, too.

"Biscuits smell good, Mame."

She wiped her hands on a dishtowel. "Want biscuits an' gravy or biscuits, butter an' sorghum?"

"Believe I'll have the biscuits an' gravy, you don't mind."

"Thought as much."

She set a plate in front of him with two opened biscuits an' poured a bunch of the hot gravy over 'em like she done for Don, Hubert, me, an Bobby. He leaned forward an' smelled.

"Ooowee, Mame, you make the best biscuits an' sausage gravy in the state."

Grandma looked over her shoulder. "Just the state?"

He grinned. "Well, I don't get out of the county much these days."

"Uh-huh."

Mama handed him a fork an' a napkin. "The coroner and the preacher going to visit the Cade's and Harker's this morning?"

The sheriff swallowed a big forkful an' shook his head. "Um-um, melts in your mouth."

He looked up at mama. He'd known her before daddy an' her got married when she was a little girl.

"They're on their way as we speak, Vertis…Sure don't envy them the job."

Mama squeezed her lips. "No, I suppose not. Can't think of anything much worse than losing one of your own…Mama and I are taking food over and wanted to be sure they'd been told and counseled by the parson before we went."

He nodded between bites. "Uh-huh, that would be prudent."

"We'll wait till just after noon before we go over," said grandma.

The sheriff picked another biscuit from the stack on the plate in the center of the table, wiped the rest of the gravy from his plate an' stuck it in his mouth. "Waste not, want not."

Tiny looked up at mama as she picked up his plate to take it to the sink. "He didn't leave you any, honey." Tiny cocked her head, looked at the sheriff an' whined.

"You can clean my plate, Tiny." I set it on the floor by my chair. "Do a real good job an' grandma won't have to wash it."

The sheriff's eyes got real big as his head snapped up. "Do what?"

Grandpa wiped his mouth an' got to his feet. "Ready to go, Myron?"

The sheriff got up, looked at Tiny lickin' my plate, then at me, then at grandma.

She doubled over gigglin', an' then swatted me with her dishtowel.

He shook his head as he an' grandpa headed out the door to the dog run where they both grabbed their hats an' stepped out the back door.

Daddy got up, too. "Alright boys, finish your buttermilk an' let's get to it before it goes to gettin' hot."

We downed our glasses an' got up. The four of us was wearin' either blue or striped bib overalls, but no shirts an' were barefooted. Only took a few days for our feet to toughen up, 'ceptin' when the sand was real hot.

We went out the backdoor after thankin' grandma an' mama for the breakfast. I snatched a couple of the biscuits left on the table an' shoved 'em down in one of my bib pockets for later.

Grandpa's truck garden was 'cross the road to the east side of the house. Daddy had already pulled grandpa's old flatbed, two ton International Harvester truck over there. There was a bunch of bushel an' half bushel baskets on the back an' a pile of tow sacks.

We walked through the gate to the garden. Grandpa had put a hogwire fence around the four acres to keep the deer an' hogs outta the field. Didn't help much on the rabbits, though.

Me an' Hubert had our nigger-shooters in our back pockets if we saw any rabbits...Daddy said it wadn't nice to call 'em that. Said we oughta call 'em wrist rockets or slingshots on account the coloreds didn't like that word...even though they called each other that.

They were forked branches we'd cut, an' then sliced some strips from an old rubber innertube, tied the ends to the top of each fork an' tied a piece of leather, like the tongue from a old shoe, in the middle to hold a rock or a marble.

Me an Hubert could hit a bird or a rabbit evertime from thirty feet.

Daddy led us to the corn which was tall as him. He pointed at the silk on top of an ear. "Now, look here, boys, see how dark the silk is all the way down to the husk?"

We all nodded.

"That means it's ready." He took his thumb an' split the green husk a little an' showed us. "The kernels will be full an' round like this. You grab the top of the ear, snap it down an' twist it sharply. It'll break off clean. Put it in your sack an' get another…Understand?"

Hubert raised his hand. "Uncle Joe, what if the silk ain't dark all the way down?"

"Then it's not ready." He found one close by, an' opened it like the other with his thumb and showed us the kernels. "See they're not full an' round…Leave 'em be, they'll be ready in a day or two."

"What if they're too high an' we can't reach 'em, Daddy?"

"That's why you an' Hubert will lead out an' Don an' Bobby will follow behind. They'll get the top ones…ya'll get the lower ones…hear?"

We all nodded.

"Now, Bobby, you an' Foot pick a row, Don an' Hubert, one an' I'll get another…Get to the end, move over an' start back down. When your sack is half-full take it to the truck an' dump it in one of the bushel baskets…Oughta finish the corn by nine-thirty or ten, then we'll start on the tomatoes and other stuff…Okay? Don't leave any ripe ones."

THREE CREEKS

Sheriff Wilson pulled into the edge of the woods next to the trail that led down to the swimming hole. He and John got out.

"Got your .45, John?"

Big John leaned his head down, looked at the slightly shorter man from under his brows and patted the bulge on his rear.

"Just askin'."

"Ain't my first rodeo, Myron."

They made their way down the path to the swimming hole, then they turned left to head upstream on the old game trail.

They had to duck limbs from dogwood saplings growing beside the trail as they worked their way along the shadowed bank.

The sheriff pointed. “Ain’t that a small clearin’ up yonder?”

“Peers so.” John stopped and sniffed the air. “Smell that?”

The sheriff stopped and also sniffed. “Uh-oh.”

§§§

CHAPTER SIX

JOLLEY'S CHAPEL ROAD

County Coroner Doctor Ralph Duckworth and Pastor Matthew Martin of the Tabernacle of God church pulled up and stopped in front of a bare wood shotgun shack just behind Jolley's Store. It had apparently never known paint.

The shotgun shacks were reminiscent of the slave days. They were cheap, easy to build and proliferated across the south. Most were about ten feet wide and close to thirty feet long with a covered porch across the front. All the rooms were front to back, which aided in ventilation.

There were several small, dirty-faced, barefoot children playing in front and on the porch.

A skinny woman, with mousy brown, gummy hair, in a faded, threadbare, flour sack dress, was standing over a cast iron wash pot stirring some clothes in the boiling, sudsy water with a three foot piece of an old broom handle. There was a #2 galvanized washtub to her right with clean, cool well water for rinsing.

Clara Cade's worn face looked up when she saw the doctor's dark green Buick turtleback sedan stop in front of the house. She leaned the stick against the inside of the pot, wiped her hands down the dress covering her stick-thin thighs and walked toward the car.

Doctor Duckworth and Pastor Martin stepped out, removed their hats, held them in their hands and stood in front of the car as she approached.

"Preacher…Doctor, how do?"

Pastor Martin rolled his brown fedora around in both hands. "Hidy, Clara. Mind we step up on the porch out of the sun?"

She looked first at him, then at Doctor Duckworth, frowned, then nodded. "Ain't got no chairs. Ye kin sit on them apple boxes, if'n ye've a mind."

"It's all right, we'll stand." Pastor Martin looked at the doctor and pursed his lips.

Doctor Duckworth took a breath. "Miz Cade, I'm afraid we have some bad news."

"One of the boys in trouble?"

The doctor and Reverend Martin exchanged glances again.

"No, ma'am, it's your daughter…Bethany."

She put both hands on her nonexistent hips that went straight down except for the pregnancy bulge in the front. "Doc, that girl is good as gold. She…"

"No, ma'am, that's not it…Her body was pulled out of Three Creeks yesterday evenin'…I'm afraid she's dead."

Clara's face drained to a pasty white almost instantly as she staggered back and her knees began to buckle.

The doctor and the pastor each grabbed an arm to keep her from falling as a pitiful wail of anguish that seemed to come from somewhere deep inside escaped her lips.

"Ohhh, dear God, nooo. Please, Sweet Jesus, no! Not my Bethany." She sagged in their arms.

They led her to the stoop and eased her down to the top step as the kids outside all started gathering around, looking fearfully at each other. Several others peered out the battered screen door.

Doctor Duckworth handed her a handkerchief as she began to rock back and forth.

"No, no, no, please dear, God." She looked up at the two men. "Please tell me it ain't so."

Pastor Martin placed his hand on her shoulder to comfort her. She looked up at the doctor.

"How'd it happen? She drown?...Child didn't know how to swim. Don't know what she'd be a doin' down there, anyways...Tol' her to stay away from there till she learnt how."

"Uh, no, ma'am...Uh, she was murdered."

Clara's head fell back as she moaned again. "Why? Why would anyone hurt that sweet child?"

"Sheriff Wilson is workin' on that Miz Cade…There's one other thing…Bethany was also pregnant…'bout two months."

She almost passed out as Pastor Martin jerked and looked over at the doctor.

"You never told me that, Doc."

He nodded. "Thought I'd wait till we got here."

The preacher sat down beside Clara holding one of her hands and patting it. "Would you like me to pray with you, Clara?"

She nodded as she tried to catch her breath through the choking sobs as her frail body racked with grief.

Pastor Martin dropped his head and raised one hand over his head and prayed in that deep south Pentecostal style as he bounced slightly on the balls of his feet. "Our precious Heavenly Father-uh, please be with this troubled soul, Clara Cade-uh in her moment of tribulation-uh…Soothe her breakin' heart-uh with the balm only you have-uh. Take the pain as you take the sweet soul of her wonderful child, Bethany-uh, and the new life she carried within her…"

Clara moaned and choked back another cry.

"...be with the Cade family as they mourn the loss of their beloved child-uh. These things we ask in Sweet Jesus' Holy Name-uh...Amen."

"Amen," added Doctor Duckworth.

Clara's lips mouthed an 'Amen', but no sound would come out.

The pastor got to his feet, pulled out his handkerchief and wiped his sweating brow. "Now don't you worry about a thing, Miz Cade, the congregation will take care of everything."

She never looked up, just nodded, wiped her eyes and blew her nose.

"Miz Jamison said she an' her daughter, Vertis, would be over later with plenty of food for ya'll...know you won't be feelin' like fixin' for the family."

She nodded again and sniffed.

"Sheriff Wilson an' Big John may be by in a day or so to ask you some questions, if that's all right, ma'am?"

Clara looked up at the doctor. "What for?"

"Like I said, they want to find out who would or could do this to her."

She bit her thin lower lip. "Awright."

He looked at the preacher. “We best go, Matthew.”

The preacher took a breath, blew it out and nodded. “Again, we’re so sorry for your loss, Clara. May God be with you.”

Her skinny body shook with continued sobs as she mouthed a ‘Thank you’.

The doctor and Preacher Martin stepped back over to the car, got in and drove back down the dirt road.

“Wish you’d of told me about that girl being pregnant, Doctor Duckworth, kind of caught me off guard.”

“Sorry, Pastor, thought it best to wait.”

“Any surprises on the Harker girl?”

Doctor Duckworth looked over at the preacher. “I’m afraid she was also pregnant.”

THREE CREEKS

We were almost done pullin’ the corn that was ready when I saw mama an’ grandma come through the gate.

Grandma was wearin' a light blue old timey type bonnet tied under her chin. Mama didn't have nothin' on her head, said she didn't like 'em. She was carryin' a three gallon galvanized bucket. Reckon they were gonna get some stuff for the kitchen to fix for the families what were grievin'. Folks in the country always seem to do that.

They headed to the okra rows where grandma took a parin' knife from her apron pocket an' went to cuttin' okra from the stalks an' puttin' 'em in the front of her apron she held out.

Mama stepped over to the tomater rows an' went to pickin' some ripe ones an' puttin' 'em in the bucket. She picked some really nice ones, an' then walked over so's grandma could empty her apron.

Had my sack purtnear half-full an' headed toward grandpa's truck to dump it, but decided to swing by the tomater row to say hidy to mama an' grab me a ripe tomater. Ain't nothin' better than a big ol' ripe home grown tomater to eat right off the vine.

"Hidy, Mama, ya'll gatherin' some stuff for those families?"

"We are, Foot, how're ya'll comin'?"

"Fair to middlin', I guess." I'd heard grandpa say that, not sure exactly what it means, but thought it sounded real grownup.

I pulled a ripe tomater 'bout the size of a baseball an' bit into the side. The sweet juice dribbled down on my chest an' run inside my overalls…actually felt kinda good an' oh, Lordy, did it taste good, even without salt. I finished it an' chunked the stem away as I got to the truck to dump my corn.

Don was up on the flatbed emptyin' his an' Hubert's sacks so I just handed mine up to him as I swallered the last of the tomater an' wiped my mouth.

"Maters good?"

I looked up at him. "Dang straight, you know they are."

"Gotta get me one. 'Spect we'll head there next." He looked up as daddy walked up with an almost full sack an' set it up on the truck bed. "That right, Uncle Joe?"

"What's that, Don?"

"Gonna start on the maters next?"

"Squash, then the tomatoes…Okra an' cucumbers last."

THREE CREEKS

John looked at the sheriff as he pulled his .45 from his back pocket and thumbed the hammer back. “No question, Myron, mash an’ wood smoke.”

“Shine still somewhere in here.” He wet a finger and held it up in the air. “Comin’ from the south.”

“Wouldn’t be so quick to judge. Smells can spread here in the bottoms. Any direction but north, to my mind.”

“You’d know better’n me…Why I wish you were still on the payroll.”

“Maybe when the growin’ season’s over, we’ll talk about it.”

A fox squirrel peeked over the top of a big limb sticking out from a hickory, fussed at them as they eased past under his tree.

The sheriff pulled his .38 and nodded to John to lead out.

John pointed to his left and touched his nose to indicate the smell was stronger that way.

They moved forward further and stopped at the edge of a thick copse of persimmon trees. Big John indicated a copper cooker he could see a piece of through the foliage. The smoke from the fire underneath filtered its way through the leaves and branches overhead.

He pointed for the sheriff to ease further to the left while he worked his way between the persimmons. Big as he was, he could move through the woods like a wraith—the result of years of hunting.

John moved up behind a big red oak at the edge of the small clearing. Simultaneously, Sheriff Wilson stepped out from a pecan tree on the other side.

"All right boys, party's over."

The three men spun around at the sound of Sheriff Wilson's voice. The youngest of the three—all of them were dressed in bib overalls and either felt or straw fedoras—reached for a double barreled shotgun leaning against a stack of firewood next to several cardboard boxes of gallon jugs.

He froze like a statue as Big John's voice resonated, not with volume, but with authority and unquestioned intent, in the stillness of the deep

Arkansas piney woods from the other side of the clearing.

"Touch that boomstick an' you're dead where you stand."

§§§

CHAPTER SEVEN

NEW HOPE

Doctor Duckworth and Reverend Martin glanced at each other as they drove away from the Harker home near the rural community of New Hope only a mile from Jolley's Chapel.

The preacher removed his hat and wiped the sweat from his brow with a now damp handkerchief. "Sure glad you don't have anymore families to see today, Ralph…Don't think I could take another one." He wiped the sweatband inside his hat. "Usually only get one at the time…Dealin' with distraught mommas when they first learn one of their brood is dead…'specially when they've been kilt, is not for the faint of heart."

"Know what you mean. I see death nearly every day an' normally one of the sheriff's deputies or the sheriff himself makes the call, but he an' Big John had to go out to Three Creeks to give it a good goin' over."

"They think there was somethin' to find? You know, evidence of the killer?"

"Usually there's somethin'…Evidence doesn't lie…People do."

"Who said that?"

"Sherlock Holmes, I think…Not sure. Sounds like somethin' he'd say though."

The preacher nodded. "Makes sense." He turned to stare out the open window at the passing pine trees.

"Mind we stop off down at Three Creeks? The sheriff an' Big John should still be there. Need to tell him what Sarah Harker had to say."

"Well, I…"

"Won't take long. It's on the way back to your parsonage."

Preacher Martin frowned, nodded, then turned to continue staring out the window. The wind blew the damp stringy hair loose that was stuck to his forehead.

JAMISON HOME

Me, Daddy, Bobby, Don, an' Hubert finished up the last cucumber vine an' headed back over to grandpa's truck.

There were ten bushels of roastin' ears, three half bushels of tomaters…'long with a quarter bushel of green ones.

Grandpa said he had several customers what wanted them 'cause they liked to fry 'em up…Don't like fried green tomaters near as good as fried squash an' just as soon have my tomaters sliced with a little salt on 'em.

We also had several half bushels of okra, squash, an' cucumbers.

Next week we'd be gatherin' the cantaloupes, musk melons, an' grandpa's special black diamond watermelons he'd been growin' for years…mama said.

Black diamond melons were the dark green, round, extra sweet ones, an' grandma said they were the only kind that made watermelon rind preserves worth anythin' on account of how thick the rind is…They're my favorite, even more than her fig preserves.

I like to put either one between grandma's biscuits…'Course I'll put near anythin' in one of her biscuits.

Folks had to be put on a list for grandpa's Black Diamond melons…He couldn't grow enough of 'em—were big, too. Took me an' Bobby both to carry one. 'Course grandpa could put one under each arm an' tote 'em to the truck from the field…Had one that weighed morn'n a hunderd pounds once.

I reached in the top of my overalls an' pulled out one of grandma's biscuits I'd saved from breakfast an took a bite…Like cold biscuits an' butter near as good as cold fried chicken.

"Hey, cuz, got another one of those?"

I looked over at Don as I took another bite and shook my head. "Uh-uh. Had two…Ate the other'n while ago."

"Dang. Sure looks good."

I popped the last of it in my mouth an' grinned while I chewed. "Was."

THREE CREEKS

The youngest moonshiner frozen in the position of reaching for the double barreled shotgun, glanced over his shoulder at Big John, then at the sheriff on the other side of the clearing. The other two shiners were between him and Sheriff Wilson.

His bravado overcame his good sense as he lunged for the gun, dove to the ground, and rolled over. He pointed the twelve gauge in Big John's direction as he flipped over to his stomach and pulled both triggers.

This wasn't John Jamison' first moonshine still bust and he anticipated the move. He ducked behind the three foot diameter red oak as the sixteen double ought pellets tore the bark from the side of the hundred year old tree.

Big John stepped back out and double tapped the shiner, both .45 caliber rounds entered the top of the young man's head, blowing it apart like a firecracker in a mailbox, scattering bits of skull, brain, and blood in a three foot radius.

The other two men, sensing a perceived opportunity to thwart the lawmen, pulled pistols from their overalls and started shooting.

The nearest man shot several rounds at the sheriff, missing on the first one—but the second found home.

Sheriff Wilson fell to the ground, but after putting two shots into the other man after the shiner had missed with one from his .32-20 revolver—he dropped to the dirt, dead.

John moved rapidly to his left as he fired after killing the shotgun wielding shiner and triggered two more rounds at the last man standing—the one who had shot the sheriff. Both rounds impacted him in the middle of his chest, driving him back two steps where he tumbled to the ground, face up, dropping his old Colt .44-40 revolver.

The sudden silence in the bottom was deafening. Only the stench of cordite remained in the still air.

John ran over to Sheriff Wilson who was writhing on the ground. “Myron! Where you hit?”

The long time lawman looked up with a grimace on his face. “Leg…Son of a bitch…Hurts like hell.”

Big John looked down at the spreading red stain in the middle of the sheriff's thigh. “Damn.”

Doctor Duckworth and the preacher stopped at the edge of the logging road next to the sheriff's Ford and got out. They closed the door on the doctor's Buick as the sound of a shotgun boomed through the bottom.

Nine pistol shots of various caliber rapidly followed on the heels of the twelve gauge—then silence.

“Uh-oh.” The doctor opened the back door to his car, grabbed his black bag, then slammed it shut. “Come on.”

“Shouldn't I wait up here?”

“No!…Come on.”

The two men ran as quickly as they could down to the creek and to the left in the direction of the gunfire.

The parson huffed and puffed as he tried to keep up with the doctor running along the narrow game trail that paralleled the waterway.

The still was almost a quarter mile through the woods from the swimming hole. Doctor Duckworth was winded as he burst into the clearing to see John pulling the sheriff's belt tight around his bleeding leg.

The big man looked over his shoulder at the physician. "Well, Ralph, you're timely."

The doctor took in the scene, quickly ascertaining that the three shiners were beyond help, but the sheriff was bleeding badly.

"Get out of the way, John."

He knelt down beside the wounded man and ripped the sheriff's pants away from the wound. "It hit your artery, Myron. This is gonna hurt."

"Can't hurt no more than it already does, you old quack. Do what you gotta do."

Doctor Duckworth grabbed a bottle of alcohol from his bag, poured it on the bullet wound as it pulsed blood that ran across the sheriff's leg to the ground, then he pulled on a rubber glove and poured some on his hand.

"Ahhh!" The sheriff arched his back.

The doctor looked up at John. “Pull that belt tighter when I tell you.”

Big John got back down on the ground beside the doctor as the preacher finally ran into the clearing, blowing like a freight train. He stopped, leaned over and put both hands on his knees.

The doctor shoved a gloved finger into the bullet hole. “Pull!”

Big John tightened the belt as the doctor probed with his finger. “Got it.” He reached into his bag and retrieved a pair of long straight forceps and inserted them alongside his finger. “Ah.”

The sheriff passed out.

The doctor slowly removed the forceps with a flattened .44-40 caliber slug that he dropped in his bag. He reinserted the forceps along his finger. “Loosen the belt.” He glanced at the big man. “What happened? Did they surprise ya’ll?”

John did as he was bid. Doctor Duckworth pulled his finger out—the bleeding stopped.

“No, had the drop on ‘em, but the young one over there by the woodpile thought he should oughta get to his shotgun…Time an’ effort will take care of ignorance, but stupid is forever…You gonna leave those in there?”

"Yep, leastwise till I can get him to the hospital an' in surgery so I can stitch that artery shut…Need you to go up to the sheriff's car an' use his radio to call his dispatch to send out Pete an' Charlie with the ambulance…an' tell 'em to get a hurry on. Don't want to leave that clamp on very long."

"Be right back." He got to his feet and headed off to the trail that led back to the road.

The sheriff groaned and blinked his eyes.

"How do you feel, Myron?"

The sheriff looked up at him. "Now, how the hell do you think I feel?…Like hammered duck shit, that's how. Ya'll done see the families?" He moaned. "Got anything for pain."

The doctor reached in his bag. "Here take a swallow of this."

He unscrewed the cap from the small brown bottle and held it to the sheriff's lips.

"Oh, gag…What is that? It's awful."

"You don't want to know…An' yes, tol' 'em you or John would be by to ask 'em some questions…Miz Harker did say she thought Loretta was seein' an older man, but wouldn't say who."

§§§

CHAPTER EIGHT

JAMISON HOME

Daddy pulled grandpa's truck under the shed next to the barn to keep the produce out of the sun.

Grandpa would be deliverin' all of it to his route customers in El Dorado in the mornin'—think I'll go with him.

Me an' Bobby an' my cousins walked back across the road to the house. Figured it must be gettin' close to lunch on account I was gettin' hungry.

We went in the screened-in back porch at the end of the dog run where the water shelf was so's we could warsh up.

The door to the kitchen was right beside it an' the door to the backyard on the other side was directly across—you could see all the way through. Noticed Mamie was in the backyard buildin' a fire under the warsh pot an' I could see a colored boy 'bout my age sittin' beyond her under the chinaberry tree whittlin' on a stick with a jack knife—never seen him b'fore.

"Grandma, who's that?" I pointed out the screen door.

She glanced outside. "Oh, that's Mamie's grandson…Come to live with her an' Ruben. Think his folks got killed when they crashed their automobile."

"He looks kinda lonely, just sittin' there."

"Made some fresh bread this mornin' an' I'm nearly done fixin' you boys an' your daddy some sandwiches. Go out an' see if he wants to come in for somethin' to eat."

"Yessum."

I walked past mama an' grandma in the kitchen, out the screen door, an' down the stoop.

He looked up as I ambled under the tree an' squatted down in front of him.

"Whatcha whittlin'?"

He glanced at the stick. "Oh, nothin', jest whittlin' while grandma does ya'll's warshin'."

"Name's Foot, what's yours?"

"They call me Hutch."

"My grandma tol' me to ask if you's hungry?...She's fixin' some sandwiches."

He looked at Mamie. She nodded as she poured another bucket of water in the pot.

"Always kin eat."

I cocked my head toward the back door. "Come on in, then. She'll make you warsh up 'fore givin' you a sandwich."

"That's okay."

Hutch got to his feet, folded his knife up—looked like a good Barlow to me—an' put it in his pocket. He was dressed just like us, faded blue bib overalls, no shirt, an' no shoes—gonna fit right in.

We walked in the kitchen. Everbody was already sittin' at the table with fresh sandwiches on plates in front of 'em—musta been three inches tall at least. Leftover ham, tomaters, rat cheese, bread an' butter stacker pickles, an' mayonnaise, on grandma's fresh bread—um-um, boy hidy.

She looked at the warsh stand out in the dog run an' pointed, didn't need to say nothin'.

We went out there an' warshed up good, came back in the kitchen an' I held up my hands to show grandma they were clean.

Hutch glanced at me, an' then held his up. 'Course seein' dirt on my hands was lots easier than seein' it on his, but I 'spect she could anyways—grandmas are like that.

We sat down an' Hutch just stared at the sandwich on his plate for a couple of minutes.

"Gol-uh-olee!" He looked up at grandma. "Ain't never seen a samwich that big afore, Miz Jamison…Gonna be most too big to eat." He grinned, showin' his even white teeth, 'cept for one that was kinda short as it was still growin' in. "But 'magine I kin manage."

Grandpa always had lots of hog meat put-by out in the smokehouse.

Hog killin' time was usually right after the first frost. All the neighbors would get together an' go from farm to farm doin' the killin', boilin' to remove the hair, an' then do the butcherin'.

The women folk would do most of the cuttin' up after the men dipped the carcass in a 55 gallon drum of boilin' water to remove the hair.

Didn't waste much, from the hams, the bacon an' belly, shoulders, side meat, makin' sausage, feet, for picklin'…yuk…headcheese, renderin' the fat for lard, an' even the small intestine they called chittlins—never cared much for those, though. Did like the fried strips of pig skin.

Everbody's smokehouse usually had enough pork an' sausage hangin' curin' to last till next year. Sometimes they'd put a cut up deer in there to smoke for jerky, venison sausage, an' such.

Once in a while grandpa had to do it by himself if he killed a wild hog that was gettin' in his crops—they really stink, though, 'specially the boars.

"Ya'll, this here's Hutch…Mamie's grandson." I pointed. "That's my brother, Bobby, that's cousins, Don an' Hubert, that's my daddy, an that's my mama over there with grandma."

Everbody said 'hidy' between bites.

"I looked over at him. "Is Hutch your real name?"

He shook his head an' swallowed. "Uh-uh…It's Seymour, but mama cleaned house for a lady what kept her fine china in what she called a 'hutch'?…An' mama thought I was fine, so's she started callin' me Hutch…guess it stuck."

He took another bite an' swallowed it. "What about 'Foot'? Where'd that come from?"

I told him 'bout my ancestors, Henry 'Lighthorse Harry' Lee from the Revolutionary War, an' Francis Lightfoot Lee that signed the Declaration of Independence—an' that daddy just started callin' me 'Foot', for short.

"Good thing she didn't like the lady's chifferobe." I grinned at him. "That woulda been a hard name to walk around with."

He looked at me between bites again an' raised an eyebrow. "Foot?"

We stared at each other for a minute. I shrugged, started gigglin', then he joined in an' the next thing you knew, everbody in the kitchen, 'cludin' mama, daddy, an' grandma, was gigglin'.

THREE CREEKS

Pete and Charlie entered the clearing with their litter.

Doctor Duckworth closed his bag. "I'll be right behind ya'll. Take him straight to surgery when we get there."

Pete nodded to Charlie as they set the litter on the ground next to the sheriff. He looked back up at the doctor. "The meat wagon is right behind us, Doc." He glanced at the three bodies. "You want them to go to the morgue, right?"

The doctor walked over and checked each body and nodded. "I'd say." He looked at Big John. "Know who these fellows are?"

"Yeah…" He pointed at the two older men. "The Percy brothers. Busted them before for illegal whiskey makin' an' runnin'…and the young one…" John looked at the doctor. "That's Algernon Cobb…his folks live over close to the Harkers."

The sheriff groaned as Pete and Charlie lifted him up.

"You'll have to check around the still area, John, see as you can find any sign that either of the girls have been here. We need physical evidence since we're not gonna get anythin' outta them three…Ahhh, damn, boys. I ain't no sack a taters, you know."

He looked to the side, groaned again as they jostled the stretcher. "Then punch some holes in that cooker, tump it over, an' take what product is already bottled up to my car for evidence…Come back later an' work it over with an axe. There may be others involved…Looks like you'll have to run the parson home. Just keep my car at your house…Get it when they let me out of the hospital."

"Which will be a while, you old goat. You're not goin' anywhere till I say so…Bled to death if I didn't get here when I did." Doctor Duckworth strode alongside Pete and Charlie with the litter.

"The hell you say…Damn quack."

"You'll think quack when I have to dig back into your leg to sew up that artery."

"Felt like you were diggin' up potatoes before."

"How the hell do you know, you passed out."

"Did not."

"Did too."

"Did not."

"Alright that's enough…Pete get them the hell out of here so I can do my work." John turned to the stack of boxes with the filled jugs and shook his head. "Act like a couple of old women."

"Heard that," the sheriff's voice came from up the trail.

The preacher started to step over toward John when he turned and held up his hand. "Stay put, Parson, need to check for tracks. Don't need to be addin' anymore."

"Oh, right."

Big John looked up the hill in the opposite direction from the creek. "Hmm, wonder what that is?"

He moved through the woods around fifty yards toward the open area at the top of the hill and walked out into a three acre watermelon patch.

"Well, yellameats…" John knelt down and thumped one. "Not ready yet," He glanced over at a set of tire tracks running around the tree line from across the patch. *'Nother road over there...How they've been gettin' in an' out. Gotta find out who it belongs to. Whoever it is has gotta know who was runnin' the still.*

He turned and went back through the woods down to the still. The preacher was still standing where he left him.

"Find anything?"

"Just a watermelon patch."

John started scanning the ground as he heard the men from the meat wagon coming through the woods along the trail from the swimming hole. He looked up and held his hand out as the two men entered the clearing for them to stop.

"Let me finish checkin' for tracks, boys, 'fore ya'll come in stompin' around. Won't take long. Don't think your customers are goin' anyplace."

"What ever you say, Big John." The man in front took a pack of Camels out of his pocket, shook one loose an' lit it with his Zippo.

Both were wearing white pants and tops.

John knelt down and studied the ground for a long moment. "Well, well."

"Find something, John?" The preacher tried to see from where he was.

Without looking up, John nodded slowly. “Could be…Just could be.”

§§§

CHAPTER NINE

JAMISON HOME

We finished off our buttermilk an' I looked up at grandma. "Sure was good, Grandma, can me an' Hutch be excused?"

She looked at daddy. "The boys got any more chores to do, Joe?"

He shook his head. "Not that I know of, Mame.

I'm gonna go out an' organize John's produce for him but that's a one man job."

Grandma wiped her hands on a dishtowel. "Somebody needs to clean Sally's stall. I'm sure it got messed while John was milkin' this mornin'."

Don got to his feet an' wiped his mouth with his arm. "We wanna go down to the pond an' go fishin' or shoot some turtles." He looked at me an Hutch. "Ya'll can come if you're a mind."

Bobby looked over to Don. "Let's just us go, Don, they're babies. We got things to do."

Hubert jumped up an' glared at Bobby. "I ain't as old as Foot an' I'm goin. Can out fish you an' Don any day."

"Hubert an' I always go together."

Bobby shrugged his shoulders. We never did get along that much, but I still loved him—he was my brother.

I glanced at Hutch. "You wanna play some mumbley peg?" I looked up at grandma, an' then back at him. "Loser has to clean the stall."

Hutch nodded. "Fine by me."

She nodded. "Ya'll work it out…Gonna be churnin' today's milk later…Was going to bake some sugar cookies…if somebody wants to churn for me."

Me an' Hutch exchanged quick glances again. "We can do that." I grinned at Hutch. "Do love grandma's sugar cookies."

We jumped up an' ran down the dog run to the front door.

Mama yelled after us, "Don't let the screen door sla…"

But it was too late as it banged behind us. We ran out to a shady spot under one of the big sycamore trees out front an' found a good place to play.

Grandma had swept the yard yesterd'y with her brush broom. Wasn't no such thing as growin' grass under the shady sycamores, so grandma swept the sandy ground in front of the house just like a floor.

I drew a circle in the packed sand 'bout a foot across—knife has to stick in the circle. If it don't stick, the other fella gets to go.

I got out my three blade Old Timer knife an' Hutch his two blade Barlow. We both opened the big blade.

I held my fist out. "Most fingers goes last."

He nodded an' we shook our fists like hammers three times an' on the fourth, opened our hands to fingers—Hutch had two, I had three.

"Awright, go ahead."

He put the point of the knife in the palm of his hand an' his finger on the top. "'Round the world."

Hutch flipped it off his hand an' it stuck in the circle. He grabbed it, put the point on his elbow an' did it again. "Johnny jumped the fence."

It stuck in the middle. Then he put the point on his shoulder. "Two eyed Jenny." He flipped it—didn't stick.

"My turn."

The next player has to start where the last one left off. I put the point on the top of my shoulder an' flipped. It stuck near the middle. Next was on the top of my head. "Curdle the milk." It stuck, but just out of the circle—dang.

THREE CREEKS

John stood and walked slowly toward the creek nearly ten yards from the clearing following the barefoot tracks and shoe prints he found.

He glanced back at the feet of the three bodies. *All wearin' boots…these are brogans.*

At the bank, the dirt and leaves showed signs of being disturbed. *A struggle. This is where it happened…least to one of 'em.*

John looked around a little more, but there was no more sign. He squatted down and studied the murky water slowly moving from his left to his right—the direction of the swimming hole. After a few moments, he ended his reverie, got to his feet and headed back to the still.

"Okay, boys, you can take 'em now."

"Gonna be 'bout an hour, John. Gotta make three trips up to the wagon," said one of the men.

"Be fine. I gotta take care of that cooker, anyway. Got two cases of gallon jugs of shine need to get to my car. Might have you boys put it on your stretcher for one extra trip…you don't mind."

"Glad to help, John."

"Take this one first." He pointed to the body nearest the cooker.

"You got it."

They loaded the first of the Percy boys on the litter and headed back to the trail.

John walked up to the big copper kettle with the pipe running out of the top and over to a cooling vat in a tub of water. From there a coiled copper tube ran over to a table where a half-filled glass jug sat underneath the end.

He held a finger under the end of the quarter-inch tubing, caught a drop of the white lightning and placed it on his tongue.

John closed one eye and winced. "Um…Stout…Good corn mash."

He calmly kicked at the cooker with his size fourteen Thomas Jefferson brogan. It tottered, then fell to the side sloshing out the hot mash on the ground. Sparks swirled up in the air from the dying fire underneath.

John pulled his .45 from his pocket and cranked two rounds in the bottom of the copper kettle. They exited out the top side into the ground creating two more larger holes.

"Won't be usin' that one again." He popped the magazine from the grip. "One left. What I thought…Gotta be sure to reload when I get to the house." He slammed it back in.

No one noticed the set of brown eyes glaring at the scene through the dense foliage of a cedar tree a little upstream of the clearing.

The preacher squatted down where he stood and rolled his hat around in his hands watching John do his thing.

"Find anything down to the creek?"

John nodded. "Yeah, I did."

The two attendants from the hospital reentered the clearing with their stretcher.

John looked over at them. "You boys mind going ahead an' loadin' those two cases of jugs there an' takin' 'em up to the sheriff's car?"

"Sure thing John." The man glanced over at the still. "What about that half-full jug there?"

"Oh, right. Well pour that out for me…" He got a half grin on his face. "…when you're done. I won't be needin' it…Ya'll handle that for me?"

The two men exchanged glances. "You bet. We'll…uh, get rid of it for you."

"Thought you might…You ready to go, Preacher?"

"Whenever you are, John."

The attendants loaded the two full boxes of shine on the stretcher. John and the parson followed them up the trail to the car.

He popped the latch on the turtle hull so the men could set the boxes inside.

"Much obliged, fellas. Appreciate the extra work, too...Put in a good word for you at the hospital."

"Anytime."

They looked at each other again, picked up the litter and headed back down to the still as John and the preacher got in the sheriff's Ford. He started up, put it in first, and drove off.

Reverend Martin glanced over at John as he pulled out on the Haynesville Road and shifted to third. "You really think those men will pour that alcohol on the ground?"

John just looked at him with a smirk. "What do you think?"

"Oh."

"Where do you live, Preacher?"

"The parsonage for the Tabernacle of God church north of Jolley's Chapel 'bout a quarter mile."

"Ah, right. That's just past the Harker's idn't it?"

He nodded. "A little."

"I'll stop on the way back an' talk to Miz Harker 'fore I go home, then…Can't do it tomorrow, got to deliver produce to El Dorado to my customers."

JAMISON HOME

Now it was gettin' tricky. The next one was over the back an' the top of the player's head to the circle—it was my turn.

"Ha!…Looky there. Looky there. Just inside the circle…One more an' I win."

The next one had to be flipped under the leg to the circle—joy. I brought my arm around an' underneath my right leg. The knife flipped twice in the air an' landed on its side—no stick.

Hutch grinned an' took his place at the circle. He duplicated my move—ding dang, it stuck.

I frowned. "Lucky."

He grinned. "My grandpa always said it was better to be lucky than good."

"Can believe that…Well, reckon best go clean Sally's stall 'fore we have to go help grandma churn."

"I'll push the wheelbarrow, you do the pickin'."

I looked at him and grinned. "You sure you know 'nthin' 'bout machinery?"

He thumped me on the shoulder.

§§§

CHAPTER TEN

JOLLEY'S CHAPEL ROAD

Big John pulled away from the modest white frame parsonage next to the rectangular ship-lap sided white country church. There was a small cupola on the roof at the front with a six foot wooden cross atop the Pentecostal church.

The Reverend Martin watched him drive away back to the south for a moment before he went inside.

Two hundred yards down the road, John pulled up in front of an L-shaped clapboard sided house, in need of painting, parked the sheriff's Ford and got out.

A worn, slim, quite plain, woman in her forties with mousy brown hair in a bun sat on the porch in a rocker. Her eyes were visibly red from crying.

John walked up to the stoop and removed his hat. "Miz Harker, I'm John Jamison with the Sheriff's Department. Do you have a moment?"

"Know who you are, Mister Jamison. Jest as well come on up."

He replaced his hat and stepped up on the second from the top step of the stoop.

Her face was wan and pale with no expression except for the deep sadness in her red-rimmed eyes. The Pentecostals didn't believe in wearing makeup.

"Sorry for your loss, ma'am. Hope I'm not botherin' you."

"Wouldn't matter none if you was, would it?"

"Well, it might…Need to ask a couple questions."

She didn't reply, just nodded.

"Doctor Duckworth said you mentioned somethin' 'bout Loretta seein' an older man."

"Tol' him didn't know who it was."

"Yes, ma'am...Do you know how often she saw him?"

"Often 'nough to git pregnant, suppose."

"Yes, ma'am. What makes you believe it was an older man?"

She shook her head. "Just a feelin'. Wadn't like one of her schoolmates." Sarah stared off into the distance for a moment, then she looked back at John. "Had kind of a dreamy look, not infatuation...Like she looked up to 'im."

"Reckon she walked when she went to see him?"

"Didn't nobody ever pick her up."

"She hang around with the Cade girl any?"

"Ever once in a while they'd meet to do somethin' or other...'long with the Hargrave girl."

"Hargrave?"

"Ellie Hargrave...Lives over on Coletown Road somewheres....Her daddy works for Lion Oil in El Dorado...one of their fillin' stations."

John nodded and jotted down what she had said in a small notebook, put it in his front bib pocket. He touched his hat brim.

"Much obliged, Miz Harker."

He turned, got back in the car, started up, and drove away. *Time to head to the house. Check on the Hargrave girl later, see what she knows.*

JAMISON HOME

I was takin' the first turn at the churn. Me an' Hutch were on the front porch to the right of the door. It was cooler on the porch than the house.

Mama an' Jessie was on the other side cuttin' corn off'n the cob for grandma to put by in Mason jars after she blanched it. Jessie was shuckin' an' mama was cuttin'—hmm, sounds almost like a country hillbilly song.

Grandma's ceramic churn was 'bout thirty inches or so tall an' big around as grandpa's hat—had some kinda design on the side, but I couldn't tell what it was. He had carved a wood lid with a hole in the middle for the dasher made from a one inch thick plank of cedar. The handle an’ the crossed dasher he whittled out of hickory.

Grandma had skimmed the cream from ‘bout half of the milk she had from Sally. The rest she saved in the ice box for drinkin’ milk an’ cookin’—mostly drinkin’, though. Their cow was a Guernsey an’ made a lot of cream in her milk. What they call ‘raw’ milk was bunches better’n that pasteurized stuff back home.

Takes ‘bout thirty er forty minutes of churnin’—that’s splashin’ the dasher up an’ down in the cream inside to make the butter clump up together.

Grandma likes to stop a little short of finishin’ so’s what’s left turns into a thicker, richer, buttermilk. She thinks it makes better biscuits that way an’ I dang sure gotta agree with that, plus I like to drink it better’n regular sweet milk, anyway.

Tiny was lying beside the churn to lick up any thing that splashed out from around the hole to the porch.

Me an’ Hutch looked up as grandpa pulled up out front next to daddy’s car under the trees, stopped an’ got out.

I looked at Hutch. “Here, you take it, gotta give grandpa a hug when he gets up on the porch.”

We switched places an’ I hugged grandpa ‘round the waist after he climbed the stoop. Tiny danced at his feet, wigglin’ for attention.

“Hidy, Foot…Tiny. Mame got ya’ll workin’ I see…must be bakin’ cookies…Who’s this?” He looked down at Hutch as the dasher was goin’ ker-splunch…ker-splunch.

“Grandpa, this here’s Hutch, he’s Mamie’s grandson. Hutch ain’t his real name, but it’s better’n Chifferobe.”

He frowned an’ looked at me quizzically as he held out his huge hand to shake Hutch’s little one.

“Just a joke ‘tween me an’ Hutch.” I grinned as Hutch kicked at me.

Grandpa just shook his head, looked at mama an’ Jessie. “Looks like Mame’s got everybody workin’. Joe an’ the boys musta picked a lot of corn.”

Mama grinned an’ glanced off to her left. “And we’ve got another bushel to go, yet.”

“Hope she’s puttin’ up some of it as creamed corn.”

Mama glanced at Jessie.

"Said she was, Granddaddy."

"Knows me too well."

Daddy came back out of the door. He was gonna carry the shucks out to the barn for Sally an' Ted, grandpa's big plow mule—they kinda like 'em, 'specially when they're fresh.

"How'd it go, John?"

"Won't believe, Joe." He glanced at us, then musta figured it was awright to keep talkin'.

"Ran onto a still upstream from the swimmin' hole. Had to shoot it out with the Percy boys an' a young man named Algernon Cobb…Sheriff took a hit to his leg."

Mama looked up from cuttin' corn. "What? Is he all right?"

John nodded. "Doc Duckworth showed up right as I was tryin' to stop the bleedin' an' took over. I called the hospital on the radio an' they sent an ambulance out for him…None of the moonshiners survived."

Me an' Hutch just stared at grandpa with our mouths open.

Daddy looked at grandpa's hat. "Don't believe I'd tell all that to Mame."

"How so?"

"Take your hat off…think you got a hole that wasn't there before."

He jerked his sweat-stained fedora off, looked at it, then stuck his finger through a hole on the side of the pinch in the front. "Ooh, maybe you're right." Grandpa looked at mama, then daddy. "Nope, she would know anyway. Never could lie to that woman…Best I tell her right off."

"Tell her what?"

Grandma stood at the screen door with a round tray of cookies that we could smell out on the porch.

Daddy reached back an' opened the door for her. She came out an' handed the tray to mama an' took grandpa's face in her hands." A tear rolled down her cheek.

"Mame, I…"

Grandma hugged him an' then leaned back. "John you don't have to say anything…I can read it in your eyes." She looked at him. "You had to kill someone, didn't you?"

He nodded an' sniffed. "Yessum, did…Two. The Cobb boy shot at me first, but I…"

"It's all right…Don't really want to know. You did what you had to do."

Grandpa nodded an' done somethin' I never seen him do a'fore…he cried an' held grandma tight. Thought he was goin' to squeeze the stuffin's out of her, but she was huggin' him just as tight.

Daddy, mama, an' Jessie looked at them for a moment, then at each other. Their eyes were waterin' up, too.

Me an' Hutch glanced at each other for a second, 'cause neither one of us had a clue as to what was goin' on.

Grandma stepped back, wiped her eyes with the back of her hand. "Now, you get those shoes off, husband, come in, an' I'll fix you a big glass of sweet tea and a ham sandwich."

He nodded, turned, sat down on the stoop, took his brogans off, then followed grandma into the house—he set 'em on the floor, just inside.

Grandpa opened the screendoor back up an' handed his gun to daddy—handle first. "Joe, you mind reloadin' this? Got a box of shells in the top drawer of the chest of drawers in our bedroom…There's one left in it."

Daddy took the black .45—looked heavy to me. "Sure, John. Where's your cleanin' supplies? I'll clean it first."

"There's a kit in that drawer too." He squeezed his lips. "Much obliged."

The door banged a little as he ducked back inside. Daddy hit the button on the side that released the magazine from its home in the handle. It popped out an' he looked at the metal magazine, there was nothin' in it—think grandpa tol' me one time it held seven an' one in the chamber.

Daddy pointed it up to the sky blue painted ceilin', eased the slide thing back an' a copper bullet big as my finger came flyin' out right at my face. I reached up more to keep it from hittin' me than anythin' an' caught it in the air.

He held out his hand an' I laid it in his palm—seemed really heavy.

Daddy looked at mama, then at me an' Hutch an' nodded. "A real man just walked in that house."

§§§

CHAPTER ELEVEN

JAMISON HOME

Daddy had grandpa's gun all tore apart an' layin' on a towel on a kind of end table that was on the porch to set tea or coffee on. He had brought the cleanin' kit out so's he could run that round wire brush thing in an' out the barrel an' give it a good wipin' down.

Me an' Hutch sat cross-legged on the porch watchin' 'im on 'count we had finished churnin' up grandma's butter for her.

"Where'd you know how to clean one of those, Daddy?"

He looked up from running a cotton patch through the barrel at me. "Actually, I have one, Hoss Fly. When I was tryin' to join the Marines at the first part of the war…you were only six or seven months old…bought one. Thought I might want to learn about it before I went in."

"But you didn't go though?"

He shook his head. "They wouldn't let me…said what I did was too important to the country than me bein' out on some island in the Pacific with a gun chasin' down the Japs."

"Where's your gun, now?"

Daddy looked up at me again for a moment. "In my suitcase…You know never to touch it, don't you?"

"Oh, yes, sir. It's like mama makes me an' Bobby hold our hands behind our back when we go in a store or somethin'. She tore my rear end up with a fly swatter when we got home one time I touched a toy…Won't never do that no more." I looked at Hutch. "Ever happen to you?"

"What, gettin' my rear tore up or touchin' somethin'?"

"Right…Either."

"Uh-huh. Purty reg'lar."

"Touchin' somethin' or gettin' tore up?"

"That too…'Course it only takes once. Just be glad when I git through findin' out 'bout all the things I ain't 'posed to do, say, er touch." He looked off down toward grandpa's pond, then back as a tear rolled down his cheek. "Just wish mama or daddy was still here to do it."

"Sorry 'bout your mama an' daddy…Don't Mamie give you switchin's?"

"Oh, sure…Ain't the same though." He bit his lower lip an' shook his head.

"Yeah, I know." I looked at daddy then back to him. "Your grandma don't hesitate longer'n it takes a chicken to take a breath to take a switch to any of us."

I could see daddy tryin' not to smile, listenin' to us talk about gettin' whippin's.

"You boys know why you get paddling's, don't you?"

We looked at one another an' nodded.

"Think so…Keep us from doin' somethin' that might get us hurt, bein' stupid, or havin' bad manners."

Hutch jumped in, "Bein' smart mouthed or givin' sass."

Daddy grinned. "There's a couple of things called discipline and respect that will keep you out of a world of hurt. Just watch a mama dog or cat…even a mama horse and her colt. They'll nip or bite one when they're doing something they shouldn't be doing. It's another way of showing love…understand?"

We nodded.

"Discipline will serve you well in life, boys, if it's done with love."

I looked at Hutch. "Ain't nothin' worse than mama sayin', 'Wait till your daddy gets home.'…Got all day to think 'bout it." I glanced at daddy.

He looked back at me and raised his eyebrows. "But I never spanked you or your brother in anger, did I?…Something my daddy taught me. Better to let you stew on it for a while…Then give you a hug after it's over."

Hutch smiled an' wiped the wet off his cheek. "That's the good part, Mister Joe…Gettin' the hug after the switchin'."

I shook my finger at Hutch. "An' I can tell you one thing…don't never, ever run. It ain't the smart thing to do."

Daddy nodded. "It's better to just bend over an' take it like a man…I suspect you usually know it's coming."

I grinned. "It's best all way round to don't do anythin' that will bring on a whippin' in the first place."

Hutch looked over at me. "That's 'bout the smartest thing I've heard you say since I knowed you."

"Oh, I got more of 'em."

Daddy put the gun back together, picked up the box of bullets an' started stickin' 'em in that metal magazine thing. When it was filled, he put it in the bottom of the handle an' hit it with the heel of his hand.

Me an' Hutch both jumped when it slammed home.

"That oughta do it, boys."

We looked up as a dark green, beat-up old Plymouth pickup stopped out in front of grandpa‘s house by daddy an’ the sheriff's car. There were three men standin’ up in the back, all in overalls an’ no shirts under ‘em. One of ‘em was carryin’ one of those long double barreled shotguns.

One fella got out from behind the wheel an’ walked up toward the house. Have to say he wouldn’t win no beauty contests—ugly as a bucket of slop an’ looked like he never heard of soap an’a warsh rag.

He stopped ‘bout fifteen feet from the porch. “Where’s Big John?”

Daddy got to his feet—still had grandpa‘s pistol in his hand. “Who wants to know?”

Could tell right off daddy didn’t like the guy, ‘cause he kinda squared his shoulders back.

“Mason Cobb…Now I wanna see that murderin’ bastard.”

Daddy took a step toward the front of the porch. Me an’ Hutch kinda scuttled up behind him.

“He’s busy. What do you want?”

“Git him out here.”

“Why?”

I saw the man in the back of the pickup pull the hammers back on that shotgun.

"On 'count I said so."

The screen door behind us opened an' grandpa stepped out an' stood beside daddy an' just a little in front. He reached back an' took that gun from daddy's hand.

"I'm here, Mason. What do you want?"

I backed toward the doorway, eased the screen door open an' slipped inside—ran to mama an' daddy's bedroom across the dog run from grandma an' grandpa's.

After glancin' back at the porch, I went in, found daddy's suitcase, opened it, dug around under his clothes till I found his gun like grandpa's.

I went back to the front door, snuck back through behind daddy an' pulled on the back of his pants. He glanced down, I touched his hand an' eased his gun up in it, keepin' behind him all the time.

"You kilt my boy!"

"He shot at me first, Mason."

"Don't make no never mind…Never liked you damn Jamisons, anyways. All high an' mighty. Thinkin' yer better'n everbody else."

"You know that ain't true, Mason…Your boy was breakin' the law an' he tried to kill me. I did what I had to."

"You kilt my boy!"

Daddy reached back an' made sure me an' Hutch was behind him.

Mason reached in the pocket of his overalls an' pulled out some kind of old revolver.

Grandpa raised his up an' pointed it at the man. "Mason, I'm askin' you to turn around…take your kin and go home, before somebody gets hurt."

"You kindly slippin' ain't you, big man?"

"How so?"

"Jest you an' one gun an' me an' my other sons all got irons…that's four to one."

The other two men in the back of the truck, pulled handguns from their pockets.

Daddy raised his right hand, the onc I'd slipped his gun in. "No, you're slipping, Cobb." He pointed his .45 at him, too…'Long with grandpa.

Me an' Hutch was huggin' each other.

"Looks to me like it's about even…an' we both have automatics…Ever see what these can do?"

I could see the muscles in the side of grandpa's face work up an' down. Daddy just had a kind of grin.

Grandpa glanced out of the side of his eye an' could see daddy's gun aimed at the Cobbs.

Daddy stepped up a little. "Not goin' to waste a bullet on none of you weevils, but you don't get off John's property by the time I count to five, he and I are gonna come out there an' stomp a mud hole in the bunch of you deep enough to bury a John Deere tractor in…Two…Three…"

"Hey, hey, what happened to One?"

The older guy what said his name was Mason went to backin' up.

"This ain't over, Jamison. Count on that." He pointed his finger at grandpa.

"Anytime, Cobb, anytime…Just a word of warnin', you stay away from me an' mine. Don't never want to say it again…Anything happens, anything at all, I'm comin' for you…an' ain't nothin' in this world will be able to stop me."

A smile spread across daddy's face. "And he won't be alone…You can check your souls to God, because your asses are ours."

The leader of the hillbillys wagged that finger at grandpa an' daddy as he turned around, got in his old pickup, an' spun the tires in the sand takin' off.

Grandpa watched them leave an' turned to look at daddy.

"Well, I gotta say, Joe, I'm much obliged. Wasn't sure what I was goin' to do." He looked at his gun. "Is this loaded?"

Daddy grinned. "Yep…but not chambered." He glanced down at his. "Neither is mine."

"Well, that's interestin'."

He laughed an' so did daddy.

Grandpa shook his head. "Didn't know that about you, Joe."

"What's that?"

"That you could face down a bunch of toughs like that."

Daddy grinned. "John, when you run a bunch of roughnecks on a drilling crew in the oil fields, part of the qualifications of being the driller is you better be able to whip every man under you. This looked about the same. That Cobb fellow appeared to me like a run of the mill bully an' was mostly mouth…Like we say back in Texas, all hat an' no cattle."

“He is…But, when they come here they thought they could out gun me…They didn’t count on you.”

Daddy looked down at me. “Might have been in trouble if Foot hadn’t slipped in an’ got my .45 out of my suitcase. They never saw him…Way to go, Hoss.” He rubbed the top of my burr haircut.

I looked down at my feet, not knowin’ what to say.

Hutch just stood there shakin’ his head. “Gol-uh-olee.”

Grandma, mama, an’ Jessie busted out the screen door in time to see the rear of Cobb’s truck disappear down red hill.

“What’s goin’ on out here? Who were those men, John?”

§§§

CHAPTER TWELVE

JAMISON HOME

The early mornin' sun was streamin' through the screened-in back porch an' into the kitchen while we were finishin' up breakfast.

I had bacon an' eggs with biscuits, butter an' sorghum, 'long with a big glass of buttermilk. Hutch had walked over from Mamie's house just down the red hill road ‘bout a hunderd yards an’ he had the same. He was goin’ with grandpa an’ me to El Dorado for his produce run.

Grandpa sipped the last of his coffee from his saucer, set it back down on the table an’ looked at daddy. “You want to go to town with us, Joe?”

“Naw, better pass, John, believe I’ll stick around the house pretty close. Don’t like the way that white trash that threatened you yesterday acted when they left…said it wasn’t over.”

“Got a point.” He wiped his chin an’ got to his feet.

Grandma picked up the dirty dishes from the table. “You go ahead and go with them, if you like, Joe. I can handle John’s twelve gauge almost as good as he can…Don’t mind usin’ it, if I have to, either.”

“I’m sure you can, Mame, but, I’ll hang around, all the same. May go down to the boggy area at the side of the pasture an’ dig up some worms.” He looked at me an’ Hutch. “Maybe we can go fishin’ tomorrow.”

Grandpa grinned. “That’s a good place to do it… Seen some come outta there big around as one of Foot’s fingers.”

My eyes bugged out a little. “Really?”

“Kid you not, sunshine. Pulled in some monster catfish with ‘em.”

Daddy nodded as he got up, too. “I’m about ready for a fish fry, myself.” He glanced at me. “Where’d your brother go?”

“Him an’ Don, an’ Hubert went squirrel huntin’. Left at daylight…Took Tiny with ‘em. Don thinks he can make a squirrel dog out of her.”

“I packed them some food to take with them…Some venison jerky from the smoke house and a bag of hot water cornbread.” She turned to grandpa. “Want me to pack ya’ll something, John?”

He grinned an’ glanced at me an’ Hutch. “Oh, guess not, Mame, thought I’d stop by May’s Cafe an’ get the boys a hamburger.”

“Don’t suppose you’d be gettin’ one for yourself?”

“Well, you know how May gets if I don’t order somethin’.”

“Uh-huh.” She put her hands on her skinny hips. “How long’ve we been married John L. Franklin Jamison?”

He ducked his head. “Goin’ on better’n forty years, Hon…an’ forty good ones, I might add.”

She smiled. "And you don't think I know you by now?"

He ducked his head. "Yessum, suppose you do." He looked at me an' Hutch. "You boys about ready?"

Grandpa gave grandma a hug an' a peck. "Stop on the way back an' check on Myron at the hospital. Imagine he's pretty sore today."

"Did Ralph operate on that leg yesterday afternoon?"

"Said he was soon as they got him to the hospital. Didn't want to leave that artery clamped longer than he had to…Don't reckon Myron will be in the best of moods."

Grandma stepped over to the counter to her glass cake cover, lifted the top off an' cut a big wedge of carrot cake she baked last night. She wrapped it in a sheet of wax paper.

"Here, slip him this. I'm sure he'll be gettin' hungry for something besides hospital food."

"Oh, I'll bet he'll appreciate this. Ralph told him he wouldn't be lettin' him out anytime soon."

"I suppose you're having to cover for him?"

He nodded. "Sure glad Joe, Vertis, an' the boys are here. 'Spect I'll be right busy with that chain killer case…'Course I'm glad anytime they're here."

"Any clues?"

Grandpa frowned. "Not a thing…yet." He looked at that carrot cake. "Got to get after it, though. Sure don't want to find another body."

"I saw that look. Guess you want me to wrap some for you an' the boys?"

He grinned an' winked at her.

She shook her head, turned back around, an' cut three more pieces, wrapped 'em up an' put 'em in a paper sack.

Hutch looked at me. "Ain't never had no carrot cake a'fore."

I patted his shoulder. "You're gonna think you've died an' gone to Heaven."

I took the sack from grandma an' me an' Hutch followed grandpa out the door to his truck under the shed.

We jumped in, I got shotgun as grandpa started the old International Harvester two-ton truck an' pulled out to the road. We were on the way.

Hutch bounced up an' down in the seat. "Ain't never been to El Dorado 'fore."

"It's a pretty big town. Not big as Shreveport, but bigger'n Gainesville, Texas, where I'm from."

We hadn't gone but four or five miles when we noticed a long, lanky man walkin' 'long the side of the road…He was wearin' some raggedy pants with a piece of rope tied 'round his waist holdin' 'em up, a undershirt full of holes, an' a dirty, battered old felt fedora. Name was Chesley Cade…he was Bethany's oldest brother. He kinda reminded me of Beaky Buzzard, the way he looked an' walked…Big Adams apple an' all.

Grandpa pulled the truck over alongside him an' leaned toward the passenger window. "Hey, Chesley, need a ride?"

He never slowed down, just looked over at Grandpa. "Nope, nope, thankee Mister John, but I'm kindly in a hur-ray."

"Well, alright. Take care, hear?"

"I'll be doin' it."

Grandpa had a big smile on his face an' shook his head as we drove off.

Hutch looked over at me an' grandpa with a puzzled expression. "Don't understand. He turned down ridin' on the back with all yer produce."

Grandpa glanced over at him. "Well, Hutch, ol' Chesley just doesn't trust vehicles, plus he's about two sandwiches shy of bein' a picnic."

"Huh?"

I elbowed him on the arm. "Means his bread ain't real done."

"Oh!" He nodded an' looked back out the window at Chesley just stridin' along for a minute 'fore he turned back to grandpa. "You was a deputy sheriff durin' the war, wasn't you, Mister John?"

"Was…Too old to go off to war, so thought I'd help out here at home, enforcin' the law."

"Why?"

He glanced back down at Hutch. "Well, you see, when I was a boy…oh, ten or eleven, I guess…a little older than ya'll. A deputy US Marshal came by the house…the same one we still live in…He was on the trail of some fellers that robbed a bank up in the Nations."

Hutch frowned. "What Nations? Thought we was the United States."

"We are. But back then in the late 1800s, what is now the state of Oklahoma, well, the eastern half was where they moved all the Indians from the southeast to an' it was called the Indian

Nations…just Nations for short…That's what Oklahoma means, Red Man…two Chickasaw words."

"Oh."

"Anyway, the government had a bunch of deputy marshals that patrolled it under a judge Parker…Was called 'the Hangin' Judge', cause he didn't waste no time in hangin' murderers an' the like…He said once to his marshals, 'If they won't respect the law…then, by God, we'll make 'em fear it'.

"…Wellsir, the marshal that came by the house was the first colored deputy marshal west of the Mississippi. He was known as the invincible marshal…Name was Bass Reeves."

I looked up at him. "You never told me this story, grandpa."

"You never asked about it, Foot…Anyway, he was very famous back in that time. The newspapers said he could break a brick just by spittin' on it."

"Uh-uh."

"If grandpa says it, Hutch, you can carve it in stone."

"What the newspapers said…Anyway, me bein' a young feller like ya'll, I asked him how it was that a colored was a deputy United States Marshal."

Hutch nodded. "Uh-huh? How's that, Mister John?"

"Gettin' there…He told me, 'Some folks think that because a man looks different that he is different…But, in the Nations, a man is judged by the way he does his job'. Then he said, 'The law ain't everthin' but without it, we got nothin'. Jest as well go back to livin' in caves'…I never forgot that, so when I couldn't go fight, I decided to be a 'Law'."

"Wow! Really?"

"Cross my heart an' hope to die."

Grandpa crossed his chest with a big ol' finger.

"He spent the night at our house an' he told me, my brothers an' sisters all sorts of stories out on the porch 'bout chasin' outlaws…some colored, some Indian, an' some white…Heard tell he arrested over three thousand law breakers."

"Gol-uh-olee."

Think that was Hutch's favorite sayin'.

"One of 'em was a notorious female outlaw named Belle Starr…"

"I seen a movie 'bout her starrin' Randolph Scott a year or so ago, back in Texas."

"Well, he had a warrant on Belle an' she heard about it. She went in an' gave herself up to Marshal Bud Ledbetter in Muscogee…said she didn't want Bass Reeves on her tail…That's the kind of reputation he had."

Grandpa nodded an' squeezed his lips. "The Invincible Marshal."

We both said, 'Wow', at the same time.

He looked down at us with a twinkle in his eye. "Fact is, some folks say that the Lone Ranger on the radio was patterned after Bass Reeves…but they made him a white man."

Hutch cocked his head. "How come?"

"It's just the way some folks are, bub…Maybe that'll change one day."

§§§

CHAPTER THIRTEEN

EL DORADO MEMORIAL HOSPITAL

We finished grandpa's route in 'bout three hours. Wadn't a ear of corn or a cucumber left, so we went to the hospital to visit the sheriff. Grandpa's pocket was full of cash money.

The sheriff had his leg up in the air hooked to a pully thing over the bed. Looked kinda like the block an' tackle contraption they hang hogs from a tree limb with.

"How're you feelin', Myron?"

"How the hell you think I'm feelin', John? Like a mule kicked me in the leg, then stomped on it for good measure after I was down." The sheriff looked up as Doctor Duckworth strode into the room.

"This snake oil doctor's got me strung up like a hog after the slaughter."

Ralph smiled and shook his head. "Have to elevate it to keep the swelling down…I told you, Myron."

He looked puzzled. "When?"

"Well you were still coming out from the ether…probably don't recall."

The sheriff glared at the doctor. "Cain't even get up to go pee."

"We've got that handled."

He frowned. "Yeah…I know."

Me an' Hutch looked at each other 'cause we didn't understand what they was talkin' 'bout.

"Mame sent you some of her carrot cake."

Grandpa looked at me an' I set the sack on a

little table next to the bed where his glass of water was.

The sheriff stared up at Doctor Duckworth. “If Doctor Linda Hazzard here will let me have it.”

I tugged on grandpa‘s pant leg, I was confused. “Who’s Doctor Linda Hazzard?”

Sheriff Wilson turned his head to me. “She was a quack doctor up in Minnesota that starved her patients to death because she thought fastin’ was a treatment…Known as the Starvation Doctor.” He looked up at Doctor Duckworth with a funny kind of grin, stuck his tongue out at him an’ bobbed his head once. “They put her in the big house.”

“Yes, you can have it, Myron.” The doc shook his head as he turned an’ headed toward the door. “Big baby.”

The sheriff yelled after him. “You can’t have none, either.”

Grandpa leaned back so’s he could look out the door. Guess he was makin’ sure the doctor was leavin’. He reached in his back pocket an’ pulled out a kind of silver metal lookin’ flat bottle an’ slipped it under the sheriff’s covers into his right hand.

“Found this in your glove box. Thought you might want it.”

Sheriff Wilson shook it an’ looked up at grandpa. “Full.”

“You don’t say?”

“Percy boys have anything to do with this?”

Grandpa shrugged. “Could be.”

Me an’ Hutch didn’t have a clue what they were talkin’ ‘bout…Grownup stuff, I reckon.

Grandpa put his big hand on my shoulder. “We’ll leave you to it, Myron. Looks like you might be ready for a nap.”

He nodded. “Or somethin’.”

“Check on you in a day or so…Did find out the Cade an’ Harker girls hung out with Ellie Hargrave. Talk with her after church tomorrow…Preacher Martin’s holdin’ a brush arbor meetin’ on account of the heat.”

The sheriff nodded. “’Preciate you coverin’ for me, John…Still got your badge?”

Grandpa pressed his lips together. “Yeah…In my pocket.”

“Wear it. You’re speakin’ for me till Ralph lets me out of here.”

"I'll think on it…Don't do me any favors…Puttin' a crimp in my harvestin'."

"You got Joe an' the boys to help you out."

"For about ten more days, or so, I reckon…till Joe has to go back to Texas."

"It'll work out."

"Easy for you to say…layin' on your butt there."

"You're the best man for the job…an' you know it. Just don't trust 'nbody else."

Grandpa turned me around toward the door. "Let's go boys."

We went outside, got in grandpa's truck an' drove away.

"Ya'll ready for one of May's hamburgers?"

"Yessir. I surely am."

Hutch shrugged. "Ain't never had a store bought hamburger."

Grandpa shifted into fourth gear with the shift lever stickin' up from the floorboard next to Hutch's leg. "You're in for a treat, bub."

May's Cafe was only a couple blocks from the hospital. Granpaw pulled into the front an' parked. Wadn't but one other car parked there on 'count it was after lunch. We went inside.

The lady that was behind the counter, guess it was May, was wipin' it when we went in. She looked up, an' then frowned.

"John, we don't serve his kind in here."

Grandpa kinda cocked his head. "An' what kind would that be, May?"

She pointed at Hutch. "Uh…his kind. He's a darkie."

Grandpa glanced down an' Hutch looked back up at him. "He is? Why, I hadn't noticed…We'll have three hamburgers…to go."

"Well…"

Grandpa's eyes kinda burned a hole through her, which probably wadn't too easy, 'cause she was pretty big around.

"Said, we'll have three hamburgers to go, May…Don't intend to say it again."

A older man sittin' at the counter with a cup of coffee, turned to look at grandpa, his eyes were big as saucers.

May looked down at the counter, then turned 'round to a long square window to the kitchen behind her. A feller back there wearin' what looked like a paper hat glanced back at her.

"Three to go."

"Comin' right up." He turned 'round an started doin' stuff, couldn't see what. Reckon he was makin' our hamburgers.

"We'll have three Grapettes, with that." He stepped up to the counter an' put his hand in his pocket. "What do I owe, May?"

"Be a dollar seventy-five, John."

He pulled out a dollar bill an' some change an' counted out three quarters, then he put a extry dime beside 'em. "Tip."

Looked like she kinda grit her teeth as she scooped up the money.

"Three."

The fellow in the back set three burgers on the window ledge wrapped in some kinda white paper. May put 'em in a brown paper sack an' set it on the counter 'long with three bottles of Grapette. She popped the caps off.

Grandpa picked up the sack. Handed me an' Hutch a bottle each. "Let's go boys, we'll eat on the way home."

We headed toward the door. I glanced back an' May had put her hands on her big hips an' had a frown on her face like she'd just had a dose of castor oil.

Outside I looked up at grandpa. "How come she to say she didn't serve darkies? Then change her mind?"

"Guess she got religion…or somethin'."

I could see he had a little smile on his face when he opened his door.

Hutch shook his head when he slid over to the center. "Glad she didn't fall down in the floor an' start speakin' in tongues like they do in our church when they get religion."

Grandpa an' me both chuckled.

We headed out of El Dorado south on the Haynesville Road. I dug in the sack, pulled out a burger an' gave it to Hutch, then one to grandpa, an' finally mine—had our bottles of Grapette between our legs, cold, yeah.

But the hamburgers were really good, almost good as grandmaws, 'cept they used these rolls an' grandma used her own bread.

Grandpa looked over at Hutch. "Well, bub, how'd you like it?"

A big grin spread across his face an' he just said, "Gol-uh-olee, Mister John. That was some kinda good…Thankee."

"Anytime, Hutch, glad you enjoyed it."

THREE CREEKS

We just crossed the bridge over Cornie Bayou when grandpa cocked his head an' leaned it toward his open window, then looked at his mirror on the outside. "Uh-oh."

"What is it?"

"Do believe got a flat. Must of picked up a nail somewhere, probably in town."

He pulled over to the side of the oil topped road. "Get out, boys, need a little help."

We looked at each other. Neither one of us knew squat about changin' a truck tire.

Grandpa kicked the outside tire on his side. "Yep, flat."

He reached over to a couple of chunks of railroad ties layin' on the back of his flatbed. They were 'bout eight inches or so long. He pitched 'em to the ground in front of the tire an' grabbed what he called his 'spanner' wrench. It was shaped like a cross an' had these round things on each end that were different sizes.

"Now, boys, here's what I want you to do. Each of you grab one of those blocks an' I'm goin' to get under the bed an' lift the truck up. Ya'll stack them blocks on top of one another under the axle an' I'll set the truck back down…Hear?"

We both looked at him, then at each other. Our jaws were almost touchin' our chests.

Grandpa looked at us. "Sometime today, boys, sometime today."

He got down on his knees, crawled up under the rear of the bed of the truck with his back nearly touchin' the bottom an' pulled his feet under him.

Hutch an' me scurried under the truck in front of the rear tires an' grabbed one of them blocks.

"Okay, grandpa. We're ready."

I could see him take a breath, press his back against the bottom of the bed an' pushed. He made a kind of groanin' sound an' the truck started to move.

Hutch got one block under the axle an' I scooted over a little closer. "A little more, grandpa."

He grunted again an' the truck went higher, both tires on our side was off the ground. I stacked my block on top of Hutch's.

"Okay, okay."

Grandpa eased the truck back down onto the blocks. There was 'bout a inch under the tires.

Hutch crawled back out from under the truck an' watched as grandpa got out too. "Gol-uh-olee!"

"Appreciate it, boys."

He brushed the gravel from his hands an' commenced to break the nuts holdin' the casson on. When they was all loose, he spun 'em off, pulled the tire free an' rolled it a little along the ground lookin' for the nail.

"Well, that's interestin'."

"What's that, grandpa?"

"No nail."

Grandpa laid the tire on the ground with the outside up, studied the sidewall, an' finally put his finger on a spot. "Hmm."

I bent over with my hands on my knees lookin' at the mark on the side of the tire he pointed to.

He just nodded. "Bullet."

§§§

CHAPTER FOURTEEN

JAMISON FARM

Joe shoved the pointed end of the spade into the soft moist earth, leaned the handle back to prise up a big chunk of the odoriferous, dark, damp soil and turn it upside down. He turned the spade over, hit the clump several times, breaking it apart.

Five wiggling, thick, fat, earthworms squirmed to try to withdraw back into their tunnels. Joe plucked them out of the dirt before they had the chance and dropped each into a Folgers coffee can Mame had given him.

He had filled the can half-full of the same earth he was digging in so the worms would stay alive in their familiar environment—at least until they were impaled on a hook. Sometimes he cut one in two with the spade, he left those as he knew each half would regrow what was cut off.

The red and white can had over twenty-five of the large worms, some almost five inches in length—almost enough for a trip to the creek. A few more spade-fulls should do it.

The area of almost an acre down in the far south pasture of Big John's property stayed moist even to the point of being swampy in the winter from the four natural springs down in the coolee.

John was right, they really attracted the big old blue cats, flatheads, blue gill bream, and crappie bigger than a man's hand. A good fisherman could catch a mess in a few hours with a cane pole and a bobber.

He glanced up at the sky and noticed a few thunderheads building. *May not get to go today. The rain crow I heard the other night down at Three Creeks was right…as usual.*

As if the sky gods heard his thoughts, a distant peal of thunder reached his ears.

He stuck the point of the spade just behind the last, put his foot on the top edge, pushed it deep into the ground and pulled back. There was a sucking noise from the wet soil.

Suddenly, a 'twack' sounded as a bullet hit the ground in front of him, followed nearly a second later by the crack of a .22 long rifle. He released the shovel, dropped to the almost sour-smelling ground, and pulled his .45 from his hip pocket. *Glad I thought to bring this. Figured I'd only need it for snakes, though…maybe it's the same difference.*

He scanned the trees up the rise from the coolee, and then toward the end. *Almost a second or less for the sound. Over a hundred yards away…Long shot for a .22. Impossible to tell the direction it came from down here.* He glanced at the impact crater the small bullet made—no help.

THREE CREEKS

Joe lay motionless, moving only his eyes as he searched the trees for movement or reflection. Years of hunting taught him how to see things that were out of place or didn't belong. Another rumble of thunder sounded in the distance. *Maybe I have enough worms.*

HAYNESVILLE ROAD

"Get in the truck, boys…Now! Move!"

Grandpa pulled his gun from his pocket, quickly pitched the blocks and the flat tire up on the back of the truck with his other hand, and then he jumped in the cab behind the wheel.

"Ya'll get down."

Me an' Hutch piled on top of each other in the old bench seat.

Grandpa also scrunched down as best he could an' studied the woods on the east side of the road, even back toward the bridge for a minute.

Thunder rolled in the distance as grandpa turned the key, stepped on the starter, put it in first, let out on the clutch, an' pulled back out on the road.

"Stay down till I tell you different."

He shifted into second as we both said 'yessir', an' looked at each other. It was actually kinda excitin', like bein' in a gangster movie or somethin' 'stead of grandpa's truck…it could be a stagecoach an' we're bein' shot at by outlaws er Injuns.

A couple big drops of rain hit the windshield as grandpa pulled under the shed at the house.

"Best run for the house, boys, fixin' to come a frog strangler."

I looked back at grandpa as me an' Hutch ran for the porch. He was just walkin' his normal walk. Think the rain drops was afraid to hit him 'cause the bottom didn't fall out till he stepped under the porch roof.

Daddy was already sittin' in a rocker with a Mason jar of tea.

Bobby, Don, an' Hubert came runnin' up out of the pond pasture with their guns. Don was carryin' a single barrel shotgun, Hubert a single-shot .22 an' Bobby had daddy's bolt action .22. Hubert was also carryin' a stringer of squirrels…mostly fox, there was at least one gray I could see.

The rain caught ‘em just ‘fore they got to the sycamores. Got soaked ‘tween there an’ the house. Looked like drownded rats.

“Better get some rags an’ my gun oil boys, dry an’ clean those guns. They’ll rust in a heartbeat in this weather…Man always takes care of his weapons.”

They all nodded an’ stepped over to the screen door.

“Get a pan from your grandma an’ clean those squirrels. She might want to make squirrel an’ dumplins for supper.”

A big grin crossed Don an’ the others faces…ours, too.

“Oh, wow, yessir,” he replied as he pulled the door open.

“And don’t let the screen door slam.”

“No, sir,” Hubert said on account he was last.

The rain thundered down on the tin roof, couldn’t hardly hear yourself think for a little bit till it started slackin’ up to just a steady downpour. Ain’t nothin’ more relaxin’ to me than hearin’ rain on a tin roof.

"Foot, why don't you an' Hutch go in an' bring your granddaddy a glass of tea…Think your grandmama might have made some brownies."

"Okay, Daddy." I looked at Hutch. "Race you…" I glanced at grandpa. "…after we get through the screen door, that is."

"You knuckleheads don't be runnin' in the house…your grandma might take a switch to you."

"Yessir…uh, no, sir, Grandpa."

"And see as your grandma has any clabber instead of tea."

"Yessir."

We went through the screen door an' headed down the dog run to the kitchen.

"How's come your grandpa likes clabber? That stuff gives me the willies…ain't nothin' but real thick an' chunky sour milk."

"Beats me, always has. Grandma saves some of Sally's milk for grandpa's clabber ever day or so. It's funny to watch her pour some up in one of them big mugs of hers…Plop, plop, plop as it falls into the glass…Looks to me like it oughta be eat with a spoon, 'stead of drunk."

"Way yer grandpa lifted up that truck up, maybe we might should think 'bout learnin' to drink it our ownselves?"

We stared at each other the last ten feet to the kitchen, 'fore we both shook our heads. "Uh-uh."

I elbowed Hutch in the ribs when we walked inside. "Smell that? Daddy was right…brownies."

"Uh-huh."

"How was Myron? He wake up, yet?"

"Was…Ornery as ever. Left him a little touch of the Percy boys Who Hit John…Tasted it. Pretty fair shine. Got two cases of it in the back of his car out there." He pointed at the sheriff's Ford.

"You don't say?"

John looked over his shoulder at the front door to the house. "Do say…only need one for evidence."

"Hmm."

I came out the screen door with a big goblet of white, lumpy, clabber. "Had some, grandpa…Want a brownie?"

"Well, thank you, Foot…Believe I'll pass on the brownie…watchin' my weight."

I had a handful of brownies for me an' Hutch. "Watchin' it what, Grandpa?"

Daddy sprayed tea out his nose an' coughed.

Grandpa kinda glared at him, then chuckled.

Hutch carried two pint Mason jars of buttermilk for me an' him. We sat down in rocking chairs to eat our brownies, drink our buttermilk an' listen to the rain.

"Daddy, you know grandpa picked up the back of his big truck so's me an' Hutch could put blocks under the axle? Had a flat...Got shot at."

Daddy sat up real straight. "Do what? Whoa, slow down, Hoss Fly. What's this about getting shot at? And what do you mean, 'picked up his truck'?"

"Just what I said, Daddy." I slowed down some. "Somebody took a shot at us, hit a rear tire an' it went flat. Had to change it...so grandpa picked up the truck an' me an' Hutch put blocks under it."

Hutch had a big white mustache across his upper lip. "Ain't never seen nothin' like it, Mister Joe. He got under it an' that sucker come right up off'n the ground."

Daddy looked over at grandpa. "I can believe you picking up the truck, John, but what's this about gettin' shot at?…I did too."

Then grandpa spayed clabber out in front of him. Guess it was too thick to go through his nose.

"Do what?"

§§§

CHAPTER FIFTEEN

JAMISON HOME

“What I said, John, I was diggin’ worms down in your south pasture at that spot where we always dig and a bullet hit close to my foot. That was followed less than a second later with what sounded to me like a .22 long rifle report.

Bobby, Don, an' Hubert came out the screen door. Each of 'em had a jar of tea an' a brownie.

Grandpa looked up as the door shut. "Your grandma makin' squirrel an' dumplins with your game?"

Don nodded. "Yessir, said six was just right, 'specially since five of 'em were fox squirrels."

Fox squirrels are a mite bigger'n grays.

"Good, been wantin' some squirrel an' dumplins. Glad ya'll went…Where'd you get the most of 'em?"

"This side of Uncle Dud's pond…mostly," answered Hubert.

Uncle Dud actually wadn't direct kin, he was grandpa's third or fourth cousin, or somethin', but everbody called him Uncle Dud. Got a three or four acre pond in the woods on his place that joins grandpa's property on the south. The pond is spring fed an' the water's purty clear, but looks black when you stand beside it 'cause of the moss an' algae stuff on the bottom.

Daddy perked up when he heard where they were huntin'. He looked at Bobby who had carried daddy's bolt action .22 that only shoots long rifle shells.

"Say, bub, you miss any?"

Bobby looked at Don, an' then at his bare feet. "One."

Daddy an' grandpa exchanged glances.

"What direction were you shootin'? Wasn't this direction, was it?"

He looked at Don again an' thought a minute, an' then shook his head. "Uh-uh, no, sir. It was back toward the pond, wadn't it, Don?"

"Yeah, 'cause you got 'im with the second shot 'fore he could run back 'long the limb to his hole…Big ol' fox squirrel."

Grandpa glanced at daddy. "You hear a second shot, Joe?"

Daddy shook his head. "Couldn't have been Bobby, with only one shot…Never heard any others at all from that way till that one."

"We got 'em all right after it started thunderin'," commented Don.

Daddy nodded. "And I left right after the first roll. Figured I best get out of that boggy slew before the rain got there."

Grandpa downed the last of his clabber an' set the goblet on the porch next to his rocker.

"Leaves it open then on that shot."

Bobby looked at daddy an' grandpa. "What are ya'll talkin' 'bout?"

"Grandpa an' daddy both got shot at."

Don, Bobby, an' Hubert all looked at me, then at daddy an' grandpa.

"Ya'll are funnin', right?"

Me an' Hutch both shook our heads.

"Uh-uh…Kid you not, big brother."

"Dang…an' the sheriff's in the hospital."

"Oh, that reminds me." I turned to daddy. "Did grandpa tell you that a famous deputy United States Marshal stayed in you an' mama's bedroom back when he was a little boy just a little older'n me an' Hutch?"

Daddy looked back at me, then at grandpa. "No, first I heard of it…Who was it?"

"It was Marshal Bass Reeves."

"Don't think I've heard of him."

"You have, Daddy, just don't know it…He captured over three thousand outlaws up in Oklahoma when it was called the Nations."

I looked at grandpa to see if I got it right. He nodded.

"He was colored. The first colored marshal west of the Mississippi, ain't that right grandpa?"

Hutch kinda beamed.

Grandpa nodded. “What they said.”

Daddy kinda cocked his head. “Why did you say I heard of him but didn’t know it?”

Grandpa answered Daddy ‘stead of me.

“Lot’s of folks say that he was the inspiration for the radio character, the Lone Ranger.”

“Oh, how so?”

“Well, there were a lots of different things, but one, Bass was called the invincible marshal an’ you know how the Lone Ranger gives out a silver bullet to folks that help him when he’s after the outlaws?”

Daddy nodded slowly. “Yeah…and?”

Grandpa reached in the bib pocket in the front of his overalls an’ pulled out a small leather pouch. He pulled the opening strings apart, turned it upside down an’ shook it. His deputy sheriff badge fell out along with a silver dollar in his hand.

“Bass Reeves was known to hand out a silver dollar to folks that helped him.” He held up the Morgan silver dollar. “He gave this to me because my folks fed him an’ put him up for the night in that room where you an’ Vertis sleep when he passed through chasin’ a bank robber in ‘94…This one has the year I was born on it…1883." He held it out.

Daddy took it, looked it over, an' nodded. "1883…sure enough." He handed it back.

"Never failed to execute a warrant he was given. Brought 'em in, dead or alive…their choice…Said 'the law ain't everthin' but without it, we got nothin'…Jest as well go back to livin' in caves'. He's why I became a deputy sheriff durin' the war."

Grandpa fingered that dollar, rollin' it over an' over in his fingers an' stared at it for what seemed like a long time. Then he put it back in the pouch, took the badge, looked at it, an' pinned it to the front of his overalls, looked up an' nodded.

"Reckon I still got a job to do…coverin' for Myron till he gets better…an' findin' that killer."

"Think it could be those moonshiners?"

"Not ruling anybody out, yet."

Daddy shook his head. "Deputy United States Marshal Bass Reeves…Huh?"

'Bout three hours later, the rain had purty well slacked off an' the sun was peekin' out from under the clouds to the west creatin' a bright silver linin' 'long the bottom.

The ground was kinda steamin' as it heated back up.

Grandpa had already milked Sally for the evenin' when mama stuck her head out the screen door.

"Supper's on, ya'll wash up." She looked down at Hutch. "Do you want some squirrel an' dumplins, Hutch, or do you need to get home?"

"Believe I'll stay an' have some dumplins, Miz Lee, that's awright. Grandma knows where I am…Think we was havin' fried boloney an' gravy."

I punched him on the arm. "Think I'd pick the squirrel an' dumplins too."

He punched me back.

We all got up an' followed mama back down the dog run to the wash stand.

We could see grandma carryin' plates an stuff into the dinin' room while we washed.

Hutch held his up for grandma's inspection soon's we got to the table, 'fore sittin' down. She gave 'em a lookin' over, nodded, an' then looked at the rest of us grand kids with one eyebrow cocked up.

We all whipped up our hands an' turned 'em back an' forth for her. She pointed at Hubert an' nodded toward the wash stand.

He ducked his head an' ran back over to it. Gave 'em a good scrubbin' this time, dried off, an' came back in the dinin' room—hands up. She nodded an' smiled this time an' he was allowed to take his seat with us on the bench.

Grandpa bowed his head an' we all did too while he gave the blessin'.

"Our gracious Heavenly Father, we come to thee humbly to offer our thanks for your bountiful blessings. An' Lord, looks like I'm goin' to be needin' some extra special help for a little while in catching the evil person killing our young women while the sheriff is in the hospital…if it be thy will. Bless this food to the nourishment of our bodies and our bodies to thy service. These things we ask in Jesus Holy name…Amen."

Everbody followed his prayer with Amens an' went to passin' the plates of food around…'ceptin' for the squirrel an' dumplins. They were in this big what grandma called a tureen. It was too heavy to pass, so grandma spooned out plenty on each plate as it came around.

There was also fried squash an' okra, mashed taters, 'long with sliced tomaters, yeast rolls, an' hot cornbread.

Bobby, Don, an' Hubert had ice tea, while me an' Hutch had buttermilk. Grandpa had another goblet of clabber, an' mama an' daddy sweet tea. I could smell a fresh peach cobbler cookin' in the kitchen for desert. Any wonder I like to spend summers at grandma an' grandpa's.

Grandma turned to mama who was sittin' next to her. "We're goin' to have to get up early in the mornin', Vertis, to cook for the potluck after the brush arbor services in the mornin'…Thought I'd wring the necks of a couple of pullets an' fry them up, if you'll make a potato salad. Jessie is comin' down to help, too."

"Mame, these are extra special dumplins, tonight. Don't know when I've had better…Not since last time, anyway."

She looked at grandpa. "John L. Franklin, don't know if I should say thank you or throw a roll at you."

His blue eyes twinkled at her. "Well, I could use a roll."

"Oh, you."

She picked up a hot roll from the basket an' threw it at him, which wadn't easy since they sat at opposite ends of the long dinin' table. He snatched it out of the air easily, like a second baseman, in his left hand.

"That's forty-eight straight, Mame…good arm."

"Next time it may be the mashed potatoes…And what was that about havin' to catch the evil person killin' our young women while the sheriff is in the hospital?…Notice you're wearin' your badge again."

"Was goin' to talk to you about that, Mame, but it came out to the Lord first. Myron's not goin' to be out of the hospital for a while an' wants me to cover for him an' track down that killer. Says he doesn't trust anyone else."

"What about the harvest?"

Daddy looked up from his plate. "I'll be here another ten days, Mame, I can take care of the harvest, at least till we have to leave." He looked at us grand kids. "Get the boys to help."

Hutch held up his hand. “I’ll help, too, Mister Joe.”

“Thank you, Hutch. I appreciate it.” He looked at grandpa. “Watermelons be ready in about five days, right, John?”

“Should…most of ‘em.” Grandpa kinda squeezed his lips. “May have to deputize you, if I get in a tight, that all right?”

Mama looked at daddy. “Are you qualified to do that, Bob?”

Mama always called daddy, Bob, which is short for his given name of Robert, but the rest of the family used Joe—I never figured out why. Maybe I’ll ask him, or mama, one of these days.

“Vertis, the way he handled those moonshiners…he’s qualified, believe me.”

“Daddy, he’s an oil man, not a lawman.”

“I am what I have to be, honey.” He reached over an’ patted her hand an’ gave her a wink—that always got her.

Mama kinda looked at him for a long time, then went back to eatin’, but didn’t look none too happy about it.

§§§

CHAPTER SIXTEEN

JAMISON HOME

A low ground fog still laid cross grandpa's property far as I could see. The sun just topped the pine trees an' bounced off the fog nearly blindin' us.

I was helpin' grandma an' mama carry the food they had cooked for the potluck dinner we were goin' to have under the brush arbor after the services.

"How long that fog gonna stick around, you think, Grandma?"

She glanced out 'cross Sally's pasture south of the barn at the blanket of fog that looked to be ten or fifteen feet thick. Just the tops of some of the cedar trees an' wild plums down there was all I could see. Couldn't see the milk cow at all.

"Oh, 'spect the sun will burn it off in about a hour, Foot. Always like this mornin' after a rain."

We were puttin' most of the bowls, platters, an' baskets in the back seat of the sheriff's car that she an' grandpa was goin' in. Me, Bobby, mama, an' daddy were all goin' in his car—'cept Hutch…An' Tiny had to stay to the house.

Hutch was goin' to be at the colored services at their church with his grandma an' grandpa. Said he'd join up with us afterward at the potluck. Think he was lookin' to have some of grandma's fried chicken. Tol' him I'd save him a couple of pieces…maybe the back an' neck.

He thumped me, but I thumped him back.

Had to dress up for church, which just meant wear shoes, a clean white shirt, an' long pants.

It was 'bout a mile to where they had built the brush arbor. It was between the Tabernacle of God church an' Jolley's Chapel Cemetery.

Some of the men of the congregation had put the arbor up usin' pine saplin' poles for the frame an' then coverin' the top with leafy persimmon, dogwood, an' sassafras branches for shade. Whole thing smelled kinda like root beer from the sassafras.

They also whacked down the grass an' weeds with yo-yos 'fore they brought some of the pews from the church an' a bunch of wood foldin' chairs to set underneath. There was some foldin' tables at the front behind where the preacher would be for the potluck food.

Was already a bunch of covered bowls an' platters, 'long with gallon jugs of sweet tea an' lemonade on the tables when we got there.

We parked 'tween the brush arbor an' the road like everbody else. Toted the food in an' set it on one of the tables.

Only person I could see to wear a coat was Preacher Matthew Martin. Think he only wore one so's he could make a show of takin' it an' his tie off when he got wound up thumpin' his Bible.

Me an' Bobby had a bet on when he would come out of it an' his tie. Bobby said in ten minutes after he started his sermon an' I said soon's we finished the first song. We bet a RC cokecola down at Jolley's Store.

Somebody had put cardboard hand fans with popsicle sticks stapled to 'em on the pews an' each chair for the heat an' the flies. They had Peyton's Funeral Home printed on 'em with a scene of Jesus Christ prayin' in the garden. There were worn hymnals in each seat.

Two chairs up by the tables had guitars leanin' 'gainst 'em an' one didn't. Have guitar music outside 'stead of piana like they do inside. Guess it was too hard to move it out here.

Preacher Martin strode up under the arbor like he knew where he was goin' an' guess he did 'cause he stopped right in the middle at the front by the tables.

"People, people, people, gather 'round. Come in an' find a place. It's time to Praise the Lord."

Everbody meandered in under that arbor an' either stood in front of the pews or one of the chairs. Most of the older folks an' womenfolk were at the pews which were up at the front with the chairs at the back for the younger ones an' children.

There was a wide path down the middle with pews an' chairs on each side. Guess the preacher needed some way for folks to come down to the front to give their souls to God an' some way to pass the collection plate.

The preacher held his right hand high over his head. "Every head bowed an' every eye closed."

He had his worn black bound Bible in the other. "Oh, gracious sweet Jesus-uh, we come to your house today in humble worship with mixed emotions-uh. We have lost members of thy flock to minions of Satan-uh...But we know you have already accepted them to your bosom-uh...Let me hear a Praise God-uh!"

There were several loud 'Praise Gods' from the folks under the arbor.

"We come to lay our souls bare to your wonderful presence-uh...an' pray that you be with those stricken families-uh...It says in Matthew 5:4, 'Blessed are they that mourn-uh: for they shall be comforted-uh'...Guide an' protect us-uh that we may live more righteous lives-uh in thy holy service-uh. These things we pray in thy Holy Name-uh…Let me hear some Ame-ans-uh."

Near everone in the arbor had an Amen…couldn't tell if they added the uh to it or not, there was too many of 'em.

Preacher Martin peeled off his rumpled suit coat an' slung it to that third chair that was up to the front—it was empty. The other two had a couple of fellas sittin' in 'em with their guitars in their laps gettin' ready to play when he gave the word.

"Let's all turn in our hymnals to page 22 and sing, *I'll Fly Away*." He turned an' nodded to the two guitar players.

They commenced to playin' an' the preacher led off—don't think he could carry a tune in a bucket. He waved one arm like he was directin' a choir, which I kinda guess he was.

Some glad mornin' when this life is over
I'll fly away
To a home on God's celestial shore
I'll fly away
I'll fly away, oh, glory
I'll fly away
When I die, Hallelujah, by and by

I'll fly away

We went through all ten verses an' the preacher stripped his tie off an' slung it toward that chair with his coat—he missed.

I elbowed Bobby in the ribs.

Everbody was smilin' when they finished an' he announced another one.

"Page 34….*Rock-a My Soul in the Bosom of Abraham.*"

I'd heard this'n before an' the fellas with the big bass voices get to come in at the back of some of the lines—this one was bound to be a real stem winder as grandpa would say.

Rock-a my soul in the bosom of Abraham,
Rock-a my soul in the bosom of Abraham,
Oh, rock-a my soul!

The folks had put down their hymnals on 'count they didn't need 'em an' went to wavin' their arms over their heads an' doin' like the preacher was already doin'—jumpin' up an' down while they sang. We were singin' along with 'em, but weren't jumpin' up an' down.

I once was lost (I once was lost)
But now I'm found (But now I'm found)
And now my soul (And now my soul)

is Heaven bound! (Is Heaven bound!)

The men singin' the base repeats were really enjoyin' themselves.

We finally finished an' the preacher just went right into his sermon. Thought the subject was a bit odd since 'bout half the congregation had been up on their feet an' dancin.

"Brothers an' sisters-uh, we have a plague, I say a plague-uh runnin' rampant over our lands today-uh…let me hear an Ame-an-uh."

Several folks hollered out Amens.

"It's this colored music-uh…I say it's this colored music called jitterbug-uh. It's polutin' the minds an' hearts of our young-uh…It's the devil's music-uh!"

There were Amens without promptin' this time. He pounded his Bible.

"I listened to some of this jitterbug an' jazz one time an' the devil grabbed a'holt of my body-uh an' made me dance-uh!…Made me dance-uh! But not like it says in Psalm 149:3."

He pounded on his Bible again.

"'Let them praise His name with dancing'…It's a different-uh kind of dancin' that's infectin' the youth of this country-uh…an' a'causin' 'em to lust after one another-uh…an' fornicate like a bunch of common ol' yard dogs-uh!…It's time to put a stop to it!"

'Bout half the people under that brush arbor yelled out 'Amen' an' there were a few Praise Gods in there, too. People were startin' to get wound up.

"We must teach our young people how to worship our Lord God-uh the right way…Like it says in Matthew 4:4, 'But he answered and said, It is written, Man shall not live by bread alone, but by every word that proceedeth out of the mouth of God-uh.'…"

There were a whole bunch more Amens, Praise Gods, an' mor'n a few Hallelujahs…That was when it started.

Several of the older folks went to Praisin' God an' jumpin' up an' down an' wavin' their arms over their heads. Some stepped out into the aisle.

I looked around an' saw one lady fall to her knees an' commenced to speakin' in some kind of language I had never heard before. Some of her friends knelt down beside with their hands on her shoulders an' back an' yellin' up at the brush.

"Thank you, Jesus. Thank you, Jesus, Praise God, Hallelujah, an' Amen."

They went to cryin' an' I looked at grandma an' tears was comin' from her eyes, too. I was 'fraid to touch mine. Never had seen anybody get the Holy Spirit before—kinda gave me chills.

Even the preacher fell to his knees in the grass thankin' God an praisin' Jesus.

Everbody went to huggin' each other, cryin' an' laughin' at the same time an' Praisin' God. I had to take a deep breath myself. I saw what Hutch had been talkin' about. Must happen a lot at their church.

Well, everbody finally got themselves together, they passed the plate an' sang, *I Saw The Light.* The preacher gave another long prayer—said there would be a baptizin' soon an' it was all over.

The womenfolk moved to the tables with all the food, tea, an' lemonade an' went to removin' the covers so's folks could fill their plates an' go to visitin' an' eatin'.

Grandpa found the Hargraves an' went over to them. Hutch an' me was standin' purty close by on 'count he took daddy over there with him. Hutch had just walked up from the colored meetin' down the road an' had one of grandma's chicken legs in his hand.

"Benson…Mildred."

Mister Hargrave held out his hand. "John."

"Sheriff Wilson is laid up in the hospital for a while an' I'm coverin' for him till he gets out. As you may know, we're investigatin' the deaths of Bethany Cade an' Loretta Harker…"

Mildred Hargrave reached out an' grabbed grandpa's big arm with both her hands. "Oh, John, we don't know what to do."

Grandpa had a puzzled expression on his face. "I don't think I'm understanding, Mildred."

"We were goin' to try to contact Myron today, John…so, I'm glad you're here."

"Contact him about what?"

Benson an' Mildred looked at each other, she nodded at her husband to talk.

His mouthed opened, but nothin' came out an' he bit his lower lip.

Mildred looked back at granddaddy. "It's our Ellie, John…She's missin'." Her voice kinda broke. "Hadn't been home in three days."

§§§

CHAPTER SEVENTEEN

BRUSH ARBOR

Grandpa glanced at daddy, turned back to Miz Hargrave an' raised his eyebrows. "Wish you'd of come forward sooner, ma'am."

She nodded. "Would have but she's kinda run off before, but never this long…just got a bad feelin' this time."

"When she left, did she say where she was goin'?"

Mildred shook her head. "Just left with Bethany an' Loretta…they ran around a lot together."

"Did she have a boy friend or was she seein' anyone in particular?"

She glanced at her husband, Benson. "She was seein' that Cobb boy…Al…Algernon."

"Uh-oh."

I leaned over to Hutch. "Looky yonder over at the food table."

He turned his head a little. "Oh, dang, it's them Cobb men what came by Mister John's house."

I nodded. "Seen 'em givin' daddy an' grandpa the stink eye for the last ten minutes er so."

After slippin' up close to daddy, I tugged on his hand. He turned an' looked down at me. "What is it, Foot?"

"Don't look now, Daddy, but them men that came by the house been givin' you an' grandpa dirty looks."

"Saw 'em earlier, slick, thanks. They're not goin' to do anything here." He leaned toward grandpa. "John."

"I got 'em, Joe."

Grandpa turned back to the Hargraves. "Thought it might be one of the girls. The sheriff and I busted the Percy boys still and I had to shoot the Cobb boy…saw barefoot tracks near the still. It was a young girl's."

Mildred put her hand to her mouth. "Oh, my." She glanced over at the food table. "I was wonderin' why they were glarin' at you…Heard about you an' the sheriff findin' a still an' the shootin', but not who all it was."

"One of the Percys put a bullet in the sheriff's leg, that's why he's in the hospital."

"I'm so sorry, but can you help find our Ellie?"

"Do the best I can, Mildred…Is there anything you can tell me about the Cobb boy…or his family?"

She looked at her husband.

He cleared his throat, glanced at the four Cobbs, then back to grandpa. "Tried to talk her out of seein' him. Never cared for the Cobbs, they're white trash…He never showed her much respect."

Benson an' his wife looked at each other again. "The boy was rough with her, but you know how young women are."

Grandpa squeezed his lips an' nodded. "Raised two myself." He looked down at me. "One of 'em is this little feller's mama, as you know."

Miz Hargrave smiled at me. "Yes, I know Johnie Vertis…We went to school together, you remember?"

"You went to school with my mama?"

"Yes, I did." She looked up an' waved at mama across the way helpin' folks with their plates with grandma.

Mama waved back.

Grandpa took his little notebook an' a piece of a yellow pencil out of his shirt pocket.

He was wearin' a clean long sleeve white shirt an' dress pants with red suspenders over his shoulders.

"Can you tell me what Ellie was wearin' when she left with the other girls?"

She nodded. "A yellow an' white gingham sun dress with black an' white saddle shoes. She also had a little yellow bow pinned in her hair…Has red hair, you know?"

"No, ma'am. Don't recollect noticing before…but thank you."

He jotted what she said down an' nodded at the Hargraves. "If you can think of anything else, you let me know, hear?"

Miz Hargrave grabbed grandpa's arm again with both hands an' her eyes filled up. "Please find our Ellie, John…Please."

Mister Hargrave put his arm 'round her shoulders, guess 'cause she was shakin'.

Grandpa turned to daddy an' nodded at the Cobb men. "Need to go talk with Mason an' his brood." He pulled his badge from his other shirt pocket, pinned it on an' put his notebook an' pencil back in his pocket.

Daddy cocked his head a bit. "Lead on."

Me an' Hutch tagged 'long behind grandpa an' daddy 'bout five feet hopin' they wouldn't notice.

Grandpa stopped in front of that Mason Cobb fella—reckon he was the daddy of the other three. They all kinda looked alike, 'cept they was a bunch younger'n him an' not quite as ugly.

"Mason, need to have a word with you."

"What for?"

"You want to step over yonder away from the crowd?"

"Don't think so…Got nothin' to say to you."

Grandpa kinda grinned at him. “Well, give you a choice, Mason…we can talk about your moonshine operation right here or we can step over yonder away from all the folks…”

“Said got nothin’ to say to you.”

“…or your other choice is I can haul you an’ these boys in to the sheriff’s station in El Dorado…I’m the actin’ sheriff right now.”

Mister Cobb’s eyes darted down to grandpa‘s badge, then at daddy, then back up at grandpa.

“You think you can take us in to town?”

“Oh, no think to it, Mason…You get to choose.” Grandpa‘s eyes kinda squinted. “If I have to haul ya’ll in to town, won’t be none to gentle about it…Just so you know.”

Daddy got the same kinda grin on his face as grandpa—think he was enjoyin’ what was goin’ on.

Mister Cobb glanced around sorta nervous-like an’ finally settlin’ back on grandpa an’ daddy.

“Reckon we can step over yonder. No need in causin’ a ruckus at the church meetin’.”

They walked over underneath the spread out limbs of a big ol’ burr oak to get out of the sun.

Hutch an’ me looked at one another tryin’ to figure out how to get close enough to hear without bein' seen. There wadn't nothin' 'tween that tree an' the brush arbor but grass.

"Let's go 'round, Hutch, an' we can come up behind that tree. It's big enough to hide the both of us."

He nodded an' we took off toward the road so's we could duck back into the trees this side of the cemetery.

We circled through the pine an' dogwood trees an' came up with that burr oak 'tween us an' grandpa an' them. The Cobb daddy sounded right mad.

"The hell you say! You shot my boy down in cold blood! Murderin' bast…"

Could hear what sounded like a shirt bein' tore so I laid down on the ground next to that thick ol' trunk an' took a peek through the tall grass that grew right up 'gainst it.

Grandpa had Mister Cobb up on his tiptoes by the front of his shirt. His nose wadn't no mor'n a inch from Cobb's.

Daddy was pointin' a finger at one of his boys that was standin' the closest like he was tellin' him to stay put…I'd seen him do that before…at me—recognized it right off.

"You finish that word, Cobb, an' you won't be able to eat solid food much less talk for a month. I don't tolerate it...Understand?"

"Yeah."

"Yeah, what?"

"Yeah, I understand, Deputy Jamison."

Grandpa turnedaloose of him an' he nearly fell down, but one of his boys caught 'im when he staggered backwards.

"Now ya'll were operating an illegal still in Union County an' I want to know what that Hargrave girl was doin' there an' what happened to her, the Cade girl, an' the Harker girl...an' I want to know right now."

"Don't know nothin' 'bout no girls. Ain't been out there in a week...Algernon an' the Percys was 'sposed to be takin' care of things...You can't prove nothin' 'bout me an' these boys bein' out there...Uh...It was the Percy's operation."

"Don't like being lied to, Mason. I'm gonna find out an' you can carve that in stone."

He poked his big ol' finger in Cobb's chest makin' a thumpin' noise. "When I do, I'm coming for you. Understand?...Now, I've already shot a couple of holes in the bottom of that cooker an' I'm fixin' to go back out there an' take a choppin' ax to it."

Mister Cobb ground his teeth an' nodded.

"And if I find you had anything to do with those girls…it's not going to be pretty." Grandpa turned to daddy. "Let's go, Joe, see if any of that food is left…Oh, by the way, Cobb, better not be anymore bullets come our way, either."

He an' daddy turned to head back to the brush arbor.

Mister Cobb just glared after them.

Daddy looked over his shoulder when they got about ten feet away an' crooked his finger at me…an' I was still layin' on the ground, peekin' 'round that tree.

§§§

CHAPTER EIGHTEEN

BRUSH ARBOR

Daddy knelt down in front of me an' Hutch when we got over to the brush arbor, but before we went under an' to the food tables.

He looked us both in the eye an' that's always kinda scary.

"Just what in the world did you two think you were doin'?"

Grandpa stepped up behind him. "They were bein' nosy, Joe. You know…We were that way when we were little, weren't we?…Know I was."

Daddy looked over his shoulder. "Yeah, guess we were, John." He turned back to us. "Need to learn to be better at hidin', boys…could get you in a world of trouble one day."

Hutch an' me glanced at each other, then back to him.

I nodded. "Yessir…we will."

"What?"

"Be more careful at hidin'." I grinned an' grabbed Hutch's arm. "Come on, let's get somethin' to eat." We took off runnin' toward the table.

"Don't run."

We threw on the brakes when we heard grandpa. Guess he's afraid we'd smooth run over some little old lady or somethin'.

We got to grandma's chicken platter an' there was only three pieces left—a back an' two necks. Serves us right, I guess. Grandpa told me once that everthin' a person does has a consequence—whatever that is.

Uncle J.B. was standin' near the tables workin' on his plate when daddy an' grandpa walked over to him.

"How's that apple pie, J.B.?"

He looked up at grandpa. "Fine as chicken teeth, Daddy…oughta try some. Think Aunt Lula made it."

"I don't know, she never could cook pie worth a flip when she was growin' up."

Grandpa didn't know Aunt Lula was standin' behind him. She slapped him on the back of the head.

"Heard that, John L. Franklin."

He turned around. "Oh, hidy, Lula…Knew you were there."

"Of course you did. You just watch your mouth, mister. You're not too old for me to still give you a whippin'."

He smiled an' pecked his older sister on the cheek. "Yessum."

Grandpa turned back to Uncle J.B. "Need to borrow your jon boat."

"My jon boat? Goin' fishin'?"

"In a manner of speakin'. Need to scour Three Creeks…got another girl missin'. The Hargrave girl."

"Want me to come along?"

Grandpa shook his head. "Joe an' I are going. If we find something…God forbid…wouldn't have room in the boat for the three of us, plus…"

"Get the idea…It's down by the barn."

Grandpa glanced at daddy. "I'll send Joe over with my truck. Ya'll can put it on the back. I have to patch a tube in one of the rear tires an' can do that while he's gone."

"Pick up a nail?"

Grandpa shook his head. "Nope, a bullet."

"Huh?"

JAMISON HOME

Hutch an' me jumped up in grandpa's truck when daddy got in an' started it up. Grandpa had the casson on the ground an' was breakin' the tire from the wheel with some kind of prybar an' a two pound hammer.

Daddy backed the truck out of the shed, put it in first an' pulled out on the sandy road with the grass in the middle down to Uncle J.B.'s place. He never even got out of second before we were there.

Uncle J.B. heard the big truck comin' an' was out by his barn waitin' to help load the jon boat on the back. He directed daddy to back up next to the shed on the side where the boat was layin' upside down.

Daddy stopped an' we all jumped out. Me an' Hutch got on each side, him with Uncle J.B. an' me with daddy an' picked the boat up. We set it on the back, though don't really think Hutch an' me were doin' much of the liftin'—did grab the two paddles layin' 'gainst the wall, though, an' put them up on the back, too.

"Bring it back later, J.B."

"Take your time." He waved as daddy pulled out on the road back down to grandpa's.

"Appreciate the help, boys."

I think daddy was just funnin' with us, though.

"What are you boys going to get into, today?"

Me an' Hutch looked at each other an' shrugged.

I shook my head. "Hadn't decided yet...Might go down to the meadow by that branch that crosses red hill road where grandpa said the Yankee soldiers camped back in that war for southern independence an' see as we can find some buckles an' stuff."

Hutch grinned. "Yeah, that sounds like fun."

"Well, stay out of trouble."

We glanced at each other again.

I nudged Hutch with my elbow. "Oh, we will."

Daddy cut his eyes back down to us, then back as he pulled up to where grandpa was finishin' fixin' that tire.

We got out an' daddy walked up to grandpa.

"You goin' to pick this truck up again, John?"

He grinned. "Think I'll pass, Joe. Back's still a mite sore. Believe I'll use that big jack over against the wall in the shed."

"Don't blame you."

"We'll get it Grandpa."

Me an' Hutch ran over to the tall truck jack. Took the both of us to tote it over to grandpa—it was heavy.

"We can handle the rest if ya'll want to get on about your rat killin'."

Wadn't sure what rats he was talkin' 'bout, but we took off anyway an' ran back up to the house. We went into the kitchen.

"Got'ny hot water cornbread patties, Grandma?" I like 'em cold 'most as much as hot.

She pointed to the glass front cabinet. "On a platter in there."

I stood on my tiptoes, grabbed two for Hutch an' two for me. We stuck 'em in our pockets.

"Be back later, Grandma."

"Ya'll goin' fishin' with Bobby an' them?"

"No, ma'am...goin' explorin'."

"Be careful."

"Yessum."

We took off down the red hill road an' stopped when we were outta sight of the house at the Yankee meadow.

Hutch looked at me an' cocked his head. "You got somethin' rattlin' 'round in yer head, don'chu? We ain't gonna look for buckles, are we?"

I shrugged. "What makes you think that?"

"Kin smell somethin' burnin'."

I whacked him on the shoulder an' he whacked me back.

We looked back up the hill. I turned to him.

"It's 'bout two miles over to Three Creeks by the roads, but I figure it's less than a mile we cut through thataway." I pointed. "Can probably beat 'em there."

"You ain't."

"I am. Wanna watch an' see ifn' grandpa an' daddy find anythin'."

"Like that Hargrave girl?"

I lifted my eyebrows a couple of times. "Maybe…Come on."

We cut off the road into the woods an' I could hear Hutch behind me.

John finished tightening the lug nuts on the wheel. "Let it down."

Joe released the catch on the jack, pushed down the long handle and let it slowly back up until both tires on the driver's side were on the ground. He laid the jack back against the wall of the shed where it was before.

John turned to him. "Got your piece?"

Joe nodded. "Plus an' extra magazine."

"Good. Shouldn't need it, but best to be safe than sorry."

"Think I've heard that before."

John grabbed his double bit ax from the shed, laid it on the back next to the boat and they both got in. He started it up, pulled out on the Hayesville Road and headed down toward the Three Creeks turn off.

The two miles went by quickly as John parked the truck at the side of the old logging road under some trees.

"Well, let's get to it."

John laid the ax in the bottom and they hauled the boat down to the creek and put it in the water. Joe got in the bow while John pushed it off, sat down on the stern thwart seat and picked up his paddle.

He dipped his paddle in the murky water on the right side as Joe served as lookout and stroked on the left. "We'll go upstream past where the still is an' then work back down."

"Going to stop off an' finish bustin' up that still?"

"Thought I would…before the Cobbs try to haul it off an' patch it up."

Joe smiled as he dipped his paddle deep, sending the flat bottomed boat skimming across the water. “Kinda hard to patch copper up after an ax job.”

Me an’ Hutch scrunched down under a big cedar tree an’ watched daddy an’ grandpa paddle past us upstream.

Hutch poked me in the ribs. “Oh, boy…Gonna be in so much trou-ble…”

“Don’t be such a sissy.”

“Won’t be able to sit down for a week.”

§§§

CHAPTER NINETEEN

THREE CREEKS

Me an' Hutch could see grandpa an' daddy through the trees as they paddled slowly upstream. We worked our way along a skinny game trail up in the trees on the far side of the creek, keepin' outta sight.

They turned the boat into a kinda clearin' on the other side that had some shiny copper lookin' equipment layin about in it. A tall pot, bigger 'round than a washtub with a cone thing on top that had some coiled tubin' stuff stickin' out, was layin' on its side next to a old campfire. I could see some holes in the flat bottom of the pot.

We crawled under a bush back downstream a ways to watch—musta been twenty yards or so. Daddy got out an' pulled the front of the little boat up on the bank so that grandpa could get out, too. He carried his choppin' ax with him.

Grandpa stepped over to that big pot an' just started swingin' that double-bit ax—split that sucker wide open.

Daddy stomped on the copper coil till it was flat as a pancake. He nodded an' turned to grandpa.

"That oughta do it."

"Believe so…Come over here, let me show you somethin'."

He was standin' near the boat an' pointed under a tree at an area that musta been protected from the rain. "What do you think?"

"Well, that's definitely a girl's footprint an' that ain't a…"

Hutch turned his head a little. "You hear that?"

"What?... Uh-uh, don't hear nothin'."

We both went back to watchin' daddy an' grandpa.

"You little shits are comin' with us."

Me an' Hutch both jumped, rolled over an' saw the Cobb bunch behind us a ways. They couldn't see daddy an' grandpa from where they were.

Hutch leaned over to me an' whispered, "Got your nigger-shooter?"

I looked at him a little surprised for a second 'fore I nodded.

"Let's let 'em have it."

We pulled 'em out, 'long with few rocks we both carried in our pockets, loaded up an' let fire.

I got one of the older boys right in the mouth, bustin' his lip an' knockin' a front tooth aflyin'.

Hutch hit another one on the cheek, makin' it bleed.

"Ow! Ow!"

I let go with another an' hit daddy Cobb in the forehead, knockin' his dirty old felt hat off an' raisin' a knot on his head size of a banty egg.

He grabbed his head an' bent over. "Ahhh…damnation!"

Hutch's rock hit one of 'em smack dab on his Adam's apple. He grabbed at his throat an' tried to hollar, but nothin' would come out but a wheeze—then trouble came to visit.

"I'm outta rocks, you?"

I glanced at Hutch. "Yeah…Run."

We jumped up an' took off back down the trail with the Cobbs right behind us.

John looked downstream and cocked his head. "What the Sam Hill is that?"

"Somebody hollerin' down around that little bend."

Then a high pitched scream split the air there in the bottom.

"That's Foot!"

"He hurtin'?"

"No, he's mad as a wet hen. Screams like that when he's mad. I can hear Hutch, too…Little turds musta followed us cross country…They're in trouble on the other side!"

Joe jumped in the front of the boat as John pushed it off. They grabbed their paddles and stroked furiously downstream.

Twenty yards later, Joe pointed. "There!...Broken branches." He turned the bow to the bank and jumped out.

John pulled the nose of the craft on up the shore and also got out.

Joe searched around the broken branches of the bush and toward the game trail. He noticed something on the narrow path, picked it up and held it toward John.

"A tobacco stained tooth...still bloody on the root."

"There's blood spatters around, too...Well, say, what's this?" John picked up a wrist rocket and held it toward Joe.

"That's Foot's. I helped him make it."

"Here's another one."

"Must belong to Hutch." Joe looked at John. "The Cobbs."

"Think so...They chased them this way after the boys got their licks in." John walked slowly along the trail looking at the signs. "Caught 'em here." He turned to his left. "Carried 'em this way."

He and Joe followed the trail through the disturbed pine needles up the slope to an abandoned logging road.

"Didn't know this was here…They got in their old truck an' headed deeper into the bottom…that way." He looked to his left, then back at Joe. "Come on, can't do anything else here, but I know someone that can help…Knows the bottom like the back of his hand."

JOLLEY'S CHAPEL

John pulled up next to a small solid concrete house that appeared to be about fourteen by twenty feet. There was one narrow window on the front next to the door—even the roof was concrete. A short cover was attached above the door header and some thick flagstone served as a step.

He and Joe got out.

"Looks like a wartime pill box."

John nodded. "Does, doesn't it."

"Who lives here?"

"The man that's going to help us find the boys…He takes care of the cemetery, digs graves an' such, an' we let him build a house here." John pointed at all the orchard trees. "Loves fruit trees…Looks like the peaches, figs, an' plums are 'bout ready to pick."

John rapped on the thick wooden door.

A trim fifty year old man with short salt and pepper hair opened it. "John! Good to see you…Come on in. Got some coffee on."

"Not for me…Joe, this is Tom Rayford. Told you about him…Tom, my son-in-law, Joe Lee."

Joe held out his hand and Tom shook it with a strong grip.

"My pleasure, Joe. Welcome to my humble abode."

Joe looked around at the sparse walls. There was a wood burning stove that served double duty—heat and cooking. A narrow bed was against one wall, plus a padded wingback chair next to a small table with a coal oil lamp beside it. Against the near wall was a small table apparently where he ate. There was another narrow window on the back wall.

An American flag was attached to one side with a wood shadow box hung next to it. Joe focused on the item under the glass cover. A wide blue ribbon with a gold star hung from the center.

“My goodness, Tom, that’s the Congressional Medal of Honor...Marine Corps version, isn’t it?”

Tom blushed and nodded. “It was just a matter of circumstance, Joe.”

“Don’t let him kid you, Joe, saved his entire unit at The Battle of Belleau Wood in WW I.”

Joe shook Tom’s hand again. “I am honored to be in your presence, sir.”

“It’s not a big thing.”

John clasped the smaller man’s shoulder. “Big enough that he’ll never pay a cent in taxes as long as he lives, plus gets a pension...only a partial payment of what this country owes him.”

“Oh, hush, John, Joe doesn’t want to hear all that...How can I help ya’ll?”

“Well, that’s why we’re here. The Cobb clan has abducted Joe’s son, my grandson, an’ his friend, a colored boy...Mamie’s grandson. Got ‘em somewhere in the bottom past Three Creeks.”

“When?”

“’Bout thirty minutes ago.”

“Then what the hell are we doin’ here?”

Tom stepped over to a cedar chest at the foot of his bunk-like bed and opened it. He lifted out a leather belt with a flap-type holster, opened it and removed a black handgun.

"That's a German Luger."

Tom nodded at Joe as he racked it partially open to check for a round in the chamber. "Took it off a German officer…he didn't need it anymore." He buckled it around his waist. "Let's go, gentlemen."

The three men piled into John's truck.

"They went up an old loggin' road on the other side of Three Creeks. I didn't even know it was there."

"I know of it, John. It's one of the oldest abandoned roads in the county…Be a tight fit for your truck."

"I'll make it fit."

"We'll have to do a mite of walkin' if they went all the way to the end near the swamp…Hear this thing comin' for a mile or so."

"Figured as much."

"Ya'll armed?"

"I've got that Colt you gave me an' Joe's got an almost identical model."

"Knowin' that Cobb bunch, 'spect we're goin' to have to get their attention. Notice you're wearin' your badge again."

"Sheriff's in the hospital. Took one to the leg when we busted a still I'm convinced belongs to old man Cobb…I'm actin' Sheriff till he gets out."

Tom grinned. "That's a good thing. May need a little protection of the law, time we're done."

THREE CREEKS BOTTOM

I looked over to the other side of the old pickup bed at Hutch as it bounced along the rutted, overgrown road. Could hear the tall grass in the middle brush over the underside of the truck. We were both tied with some dirty cotton clothesline rope—hands behind our back.

Daddy Cobb was sittin' on the side of the box above us, had a wad of tobacco in his mouth an' would spit ever once in a while out to the side. He had his hat cocked to the back so's not to mash on that knot I gave him.

"What do you want with us?…Daddy an' grandpa are gonna be comin'…Wait an' see."

He snickered an' spit a long brown stream next my head. "Ain't no never mind…Gonna teach yer grandpa a lesson he'll never fergit…He kilt my boy…Seen him do it. Pay 'im back, I am…piece at a time." He looked at Hutch with a sneer at the side of his face. "The nigger too."

§§§

CHAPTER TWENTY

THREE CREEKS BOTTOM

John turned off the Haynesville Road, drove a mile and turned again where Tom pointed.

"Durn, Tom, you sure there's a road here?"

He smiled and nodded. "You'll see it better once we get deeper into the trees…There's another way in further down, but this'll work to get us to that loggin' road you were talkin' about."

The old two-ton truck bounced and jumped on the ancient ruts as new growth saplings disappeared under the chassis in the front.

The three men jostled shoulder to shoulder as John shifted down into second gear.

Joe, in the middle, had to straddle the floor shift with it between his knees.

"Watch your hand there, John."

"You shift for me, then."

"Can do that…Say when."

John pushed the clutch in. "When…Go to first."

Joe maneuvered the tall lever back and to the far left and further back.

The transmission geared down as the engine roared and the truck slowed while it pushed a couple of larger pine saplings over with its drill stem pipe bumper.

"Back to second." John pushed the clutch in again.

Joe reversed his pattern to go back up to second. That would be as fast as they could go on this old road—actually not more that a trail, now.

“Here we go, turn right, John.”

He turned the truck onto a more used road with mature pine trees on either side—still with tall grass in the middle.

“Better, Tom…but not no hell of a lot.”

“Beggers can’t be choosers, John…Could already be walkin’.”

Joe turned to his right. “When does that start?”

“’Bout a mile.”

“We seem to be going downhill, Tom.”

“Are…Some say there are panther an’ bear down in here.”

John glanced over at him. “And?”

“Never seen any bear.”

Joe and John exchanged looks.

I glanced around at what I could see as the battered old ’39 Plymouth flathead six cylinder pickup rattled into an open area beside a spring fed branch and stopped.

Could only see the tops of tall pines mixed with some oaks, hickory, an’ sweetgum from where me an’ Hutch was in the bed of their truck.

Two of the Cobb boys got out of the cab. One of 'em was the one I knocked the tooth out with my nigger-shooter. Think his name was Harley. The other one had a mouse with a cut in the middle on his cheek from Hutch—daddy Cobb called him Jase.

There was some of that same stuff we saw granpaw an' daddy tear up back near the creek. Purty sure it was for makin' moonshine.

"Tend to that fire, Berty, it's 'bout out…Damn shore don't want to start over with that mash…wanna add some yella-meat watermelon to it from our field 'cross the creek tomorrow."

"Okay, Paw…git right on it. Love watermelon flavored shine."

His voice was still raspy from gettin' hit in the throat.

There was a stack of cut an' split logs nearby like at the other place. He commenced to stokin' the fire under that copper pot an' addin' logs.

"Harley, you an' Jase git these kids outta the truck an' over by that big pin oak by the branch…Check them ropes an' tie their feet together. Don't want 'em wanderin' off into these woods…might git lost er somethin'." He chuckled.

"…String 'em up from that limb stickin' out thisaway later."

He spit another long stream of tobacco juice off to the side an' wiped the dribble off his chin with his sleeve.

Those two Cobb boys slung me an' Hutch over their shoulders an' toted us to the tree where they dropped us. Hutch landed mostly on his face an' his nose started to bleed.

The one called Jase, took some more of that clothline rope an' tied our feet together, then walked off.

I wormed my way over next to Hutch. "You hurt?"

"Naw, just thought I'd bleed fer a while…nothin' else to do."

"Well, least your mouth still works."

Hutch nodded. "Fer now…Wonder what old man Cobb meant 'bout stringin' us up from that limb over our heads?"

"Dunno. Ain't that what they say in the cowboy movies when they're gonna hang somebody?"

"You coulda said most anythin' but that."

"Way he talked though before, he was gonna whack us up in chunks an' send piece at the time to grandpa on 'count he shot his boy."

"Yeah, he said that…Yer just full of upliftin' information, ain'tcha?"

"Hope daddy an' grandpa get here in time."

"That's the first good thing you said."

"Say, got a idea."

"Uh-oh…what now?…Your last one got us in this mess."

"Well, I'm gonna get us out, too…Which pocket is your jack knife in?"

"Uh…back, why?"

"Right or left?"

"Uh, right."

I looked over to see if I could tell where each of the Cobbs were. Seemed to all be doin' somethin' with that still.

"Work your back over to me…I'll roll over."

"For what?"

"Gonna see if I can get my hands in your back pocket."

Hutch rolled his eyes. "Oh, Lordy."

Tom glanced around. "Alright, better shut 'er down here, John. Not much difference between this truck an' a brass band."

"Leave the truck right here?"

"Yeah, they can't get around it if they try to make a run for it."

"Good idea."

They took out walking along the tire paths on the road. Tom was on the left, John and Joe on the right with the wide grass strip in between.

The old Marine glanced over at John. "I'll take point when we get a bit closer…gettin' an occasional whiff of smoke now…Got a fire goin' somewhere up ahead…Hard to tell in these woods."

"Probably another still."

"Figure…We'll slip off into the woods away from this road when I go to point 'bout a hundred yards or so out."

"It's possible there may be a young girl there, too."

Tom looked surprised. "A young girl?"

"Had several girls killed in the last week an' one missin'. Found the first two an' were lookin' for the third when the Cobbs got the boys."

"Think they're doin' it all?"

"Best suspects, so far. The youngest Cobb, the one I had to shoot when the sheriff an' I busted their still on the other side of Three Creeks, had been sparkin' the third girl…Ellie Hargrave."

"Met the Hargraves a while back. Good people…Daughter's an attractive redheaded girl 'bout fifteen, isn't she?"

"Yep, her mama says she was wearin' a yellow sun dress when she left the house with the others a few days ago…Girls hung out together an' all come up missin' at the same time."

"My son, Foot, an' I found the bodies of the other two at the swimmin' hole on Three Creeks."

Tom looked at Joe, then at John. "Cobbs would be at the top of my list, too."

"Got it."

I quickly looked up an' 'round checkin' on the whereabouts of the Cobbs. All of 'em were still busy at their chores. Daddy Cobb looked to be tastin' some of their wares.

I got the big blade open an' felt for Hutch's ropes 'round his wrists. "Hope I don't cut you."

"Already bleedin' anyways…Ain't sharpened it since we played mumbley peg."

"Oh, boy." I kinda squirmed 'round, managed to feel the rope an' went to cuttin' on it. "You're right, ain't real sharp."

I sawed on the tough cotton. Clothesline rope is hard to cut, even with a sharp knife—but got no other choice.

The regular sounds in the wood was all about. I could hear a mockin' bird goin' through the songs he stole—no idea how he remembers 'em all.

A couple of squirrels were fussin' in a hickory tree next to the pin oak me an' Hutch was under—then a red tail hawk let out with his huntin' cry overhead.

Wish that's what me an' Hutch were doin' 'stead of layin' here waitin' to get strung up—I kept cuttin'.

Then I froze.

Daddy Cobb was walkin' our way with his finger through the loop on one of his jugs. He wadn't none too steady on his feet.

He went to squat down in front of us, but fell over on his hiney an' took another pull on the jug.

"You little bastards 're fixin' to catch it."

I could hear Hutch startin' to blubber up behind me.

"Hush up, Hutch...Grandpa an' them are comin'...know they are."

Daddy Cobb had another swig.

"Don't make no never mind. Never find us back in here. No...nobody knows 'bout that ol' road 'ceptin' us."

He pulled a ugly lookin' skinnin' knife from the scabbard under the rope 'round his waist an' waved it 'round.

"Gonna string yer scrawny little asses up in this here tree an' go to skinnin' you like hogs...That big bad grandpa of yers will be gittin' some presents on his front porch...Smoked white an' dark meat."

§§§

CHAPTER TWENTY-ONE

THREE CREEKS BOTTOM

Tom held his fist up signaling John and Joe to stop. He cocked his head listening, held his finger to his lips, then pointed John to the left of the road and Joe to the right.

He pointed to himself, circled his index finger in the air and moved forward around ten yards before disappearing into the trees on the right of the road to take point.

The three men moved silently through the thick forest in the direction of the sounds from the Cobb's moonshine still area, each had his handgun at the ready.

I watched Mason Cobb get to his feet—he was more than a bit wobbly. He staggered back over to the others.

Berty was tendin' the fire again an' them other two, what grandma would call, ne'er do wells, was sittin' on the ground chewin' on some jerky. Daddy Cobb dropped to his hiney again next to 'em.

I leaned back to Hutch an' continued sawin' on his ropes till I felt one part. "Pull a bit, think I cut one."

He moved his hands back an' forth an' they came apart. "Got it."

Roll over to me an' cut mine, now…do your ankles first, though.

"Okay."

Hutch bent over an' cut his ankle rope. It's a mite easier when you can look at the rope while cuttin'.

He rolled back over an' went to sawin' on mine 'round my wrists till they parted, too. I twisted around, took his knife an' reached down to cut my ankle ropes.

"Hey! What're ya'll doin'?"

I jerked up to see Jase stompin' in our direction. "Run, Hutch, run!"

"Cain't leave you."

"Run, dang it. Find grandpa an' daddy."

He looked up as the Cobb boy started runnin' toward us an' he took off through the thick brush an' whoa vines.

"Git back here, you little spook!"

When he ran past me chasin' Hutch, I lunged forward an' grabbed his ankle on the way, spillin' him on his face in the dirt.

He jumped up, spun 'round, saw my hands was loose an' my ankle ropes were partial cut.

"Damn you."

He slapped the knife outta my hand, an' then backhanded me cross the side of my face, knockin' me arollin'. I saw stars for a couple seconds 'fore he reached down an’ drug me back to the tree an’ retied my hands with some cord he had in his pocket.

“That oughta hold yer sorry little ass.”

Time he finished, old man Cobb an’ the other two had come up.

“You fools wadn’t watchin’. Coulda lost ‘em both.”

He took his hat an’ worked the boys over with it, one at the time. Don’t think it hurt ‘em much, though.

“Bring some more of that rope from the truck, just as well string him up in this tree now…won’t be no gittin’ loose from that.” He slapped me ‘cross the face, bustin’ my lip.

Berty ran over to the truck an’ brought back a coil of that nasty lookin’ rope. He made a loop on one end an’ slipped it over my feet.

Harley took the coil from him, slung it over that big ol’ limb over his head an’ then him an’ Jace hauled me up in the air…upside down. They held the rope while Berty wrapped the rest round the trunk an’ tied it off.

It dawned on me then, I was in some kind of deep trouble now. I tried to watch what they were doin', but I was spinin' 'round an' swingin' too much.

I caught old man Cobb takin' his skinnin' knife out an' testin' the edge with his thumb on one circle out of the corner of my eye.

Hutch ran as fast as he could, zigzagging through and around the big trees and jumping over most of the berry and green whoa vines, till he tripped. He fell to his face and scrambled back to his feet only to run into a man.

He screamed and looked up.

"Shhh, hush, boy, we're here to help. You alright?"

It only took a couple of seconds for Joe to join Tom.

"Hutch, keep quiet…Tom's a friend of ours. We've come to get ya'll. Is Foot still okay?"

Hutch nodded, sucked in his breath and wiped the blood from his nose. "Was when I left. He got me cut loose an' tol' me to run. They seen him a cuttin' the ropes with my jack knife."

"You stay right here. We'll take care of it, hear? Just sit down."

He nodded and sat down with his back to a thick sweetgum.

"Lead on, Tom."

The two men headed toward the small clearing near a branch that would flow into Three Creeks. Tom pointed to his left for Joe to split off.

Old man Cobb spit a long stream of slimy tobacco juice to the side an' grinned at me showin' his rotted, yellow teeth as my swingin' an' spinnin' slowed some.

He stepped up, grabbed the front of my overalls to stop me facin' 'im…The stink comin' from him was like somethin' dead. I started cryin'…tried not to, but just couldn't help it. All I could think of was I wouldn't never see my mama an' daddy again.

I squeezed my eyes tight an' gritted my teeth at the pain I knew was comin'.

"Touch that boy with that blade an' you're dead where you stand."

It got real quiet. My eyes snapped open an' saw a man, without no hat, standin' just inside the clearin' pointin' some kinda gun at daddy Cobb. Didn't know him from Adam's ox—not sure he had one. Then I heard my daddy an' I started cryin' again.

"You step back away from him, you son of a bitch, an' drop that knife."

All of a sudden the silence that was there was gone when there were several gunshots from close by. The old man turned aloose of my overalls an' bumped past me causin' me to start spinnin' again.

My ears were ringin' as more shots were fired, 'cludin' a shotgun. I saw daddy shootin', then there was grandpa on the other side of the clearin', he was shootin', too—an' so was the man I didn't know.

The Cobb boys had started shootin' first, but they didn't count on daddy an' grandpa. I could only see things happenin' each time I spun around, not to say nothin' 'bout gettin' dizzy. Sounded like one of those shoot out scenes from a Three Mesquiteers cowboy movie—then it stopped.

I stopped spinnin' an' looked up at daddy's face as he looked down at me.

"You okay, boy?"

"Uh-huh, just dizzy."

He took his Old Grandad jack knife out an' cut the rope just above my feet while he held me with his left arm. Daddy let me down gentle like an' pulled that loop off my ankles.

I sat up an' hugged his neck.

"I was scared, Daddy, really scared."

I looked around an' saw the three Cobb boys layin' about, then grandpa walked up. The man I didn't know was behind daddy.

"Where's Hutch?"

"Right here." I turned an' he was steppin' out from behind the tree I was hangin' from.

"What is it about 'stay right here' you didn't understand, son?"

Hutch looked down at his feet then back up at daddy. "Well, you didn't say how long."

I leaned over. "Daddy, who's that man?"

"He's a friend of your grandpa. Led us here. He's an honest to God war hero. Has the Medal of Honor…name's Tom."

"Golly gee…He's the Marine that gave grandpa his gun."

Grandpa glanced at the three bodies. "Anybody see Mason?"

"He cut an' ran at the first shot, John, sorry." Tom looked off. "Ran that way, toward the thick part of the bottom."

Daddy turned to Tom. "This ain't thick?"

"Uh-uh…not compared to that way."

Grandpa nodded. "He'll show up, bad pennies usually do…Anyone see any sign of the girl?"

I looked up at him. "Wadn't no sign of anybody else when we got here, Grandpa."

He kinda set his jaw. "Well, reckon we're back to square one…Let's take care of this still while we're down here."

"There's an ax over by the stack of wood, John." Daddy walked over and picked it up.

"Best kick it over to drain all that hot mash out. Don't want to hit it with an ax while it's cookin' under pressure."

Daddy grinned. "That's a fact."

Tom stepped over to the already filled jugs. "Mind if I have one of these, John?…For medicinal purposes, you understand."

Grandpa smiled. "Yeah, good idea, Tom, never know when a fellow might get snake bit or a case of the croup…Might have to take one myself."

"Daddy, that stuff good for snakebite?"

"Well, sometimes, Hoss Fly, sometimes."

He drew back an' kicked the copper pot over, knockin' the lid with the tubin' in it off. A steamin' mess poured out that looked kinda like Malt-O-Meal, but didn't smell anything like it.

Daddy went to work with that choppin' ax after most of that stuff poured out. Tom got his jug, grandpa got one for him an' one for daddy 'fore they busted the rest of 'em up.

When daddy had finished with the ax, he turned to grandpa. "Where do we look next, John?"

He kinda arched his eyebrows. "Still need to give the creek a good goin' over…Have to eliminate it…after we take Tom and the boys home. Plus gotta stop by Smead's store an' call for the meat wagon to come out an' pick up the Cobbs."

"No need to rush, John…The boys an' I can wait at the truck or down by the creek while ya'll do your thing…No need in makin' several trips."

"Tom's got a point, John. We can use the radio in the sheriff's car to call in when we get back…'specially, uh…if we find anything in the creek."

"Yeah, guess ya'll have a point." He looked at me an' Hutch. "Alright with you boys?"

We glanced at each other an' nodded, both of us thinkin' there was maybe more adventure.

"How's your nose there, Hutch?"

"It be fine Mister John, just banged it a little."

"An' your lip, Foot?"

I tried to grin but that didn't work cause my lip was swole up. "Like daddy's told me more'n once, 'Had a worse place on my lip, boy, an' never quit whistling'…'course I ain't tried that yet."

§§§

CHAPTER TWENTY-TWO

THREE CREEKS BOTTOM

Tom led the way back to grandpa's truck. Him an' daddy sat on the bed with their backs against the cab while me an' Hutch got inside.

Grandpa had to do a bunch of backin' back an' forth till he got that big ol' truck turned around on the narrow road. We headed out the way they come in so we could get to the Haynesville Road.

"We goin' down to Three Creeks, Grandpa?"

"Yep, need to see if we can find the Hargrave girl while we're here. Got your Uncle J.B.'s jon boat. You an' Hutch can wait with Tom…maybe ya'll can get him to tell you some stories about bein' in the Marine Corps."

Me an' Hutch looked at each other an' grinned.

Grandpa pulled off the Haynesville Road onto the loggin' road that led down to the swimmin' hole. He parked an' we all got out. Daddy an' Tom had jumped off the back an' were walkin' down to the creek where Uncle J.B.'s boat was.

Daddy an' grandpa got in the flat-bottomed boat.

"We'll be back this way in a bit. Check upstream first, then come back an' go downstream a ways."

Grandpa pushed away from the bank an' he an daddy paddled to the left out of sight around the first bend.

I looked over at Tom an' pointed at his gun. "Is that a honest to gosh German pistol, Mister Rayford?"

"It is."

"Did a German give it to you?"

He kinda smiled. "In a manner of speakin', Hutch."

Me an' Hutch glanced at each other.

I frowned. "What do you mean?"

"Well, there was this battle goin' on in some woods about as thick as these over in France…The fightin' was pretty fierce, there was a lot of smoke an' I was dodgin' from tree to tree tryin' to get closer to a bunch of Germans that were shootin' at us."

"Weren't ya'll shootin' back?"

"We were, Foot, an' we were pretty well outnumbered. The commander of the French troops we were fightin' with kept tryin' to get us to retreat." Tom kinda chuckled. "My commandin' officer, Captain Lloyd Williams of the 2nd Battalion, 5th Marines told him, 'Retreat? Hell, we just got here'…Wasn't no quit in him. He was a real Marine."

Hutch was sittin' cross-legged in front of Tom, well, he looked up at him for a moment. "Mister Tom, I heard that's the way Marines are, guess that's true, huh?"

“Seems so, son, seems so…We had dug some shallow trenches in the dirt with our bayonets so we could shoot layin’ in ‘em…The Germans were rakin’ our position with machine gun fire an’ some of us, includin’ me, were out of rifle ammo. It was gettin’ right testy, don’t mind sayin’.

“I decided, ‘Well, hell, can’t live forever’, I took my pistol…”

“The one you give grandpa?”

“Yep, that one…it had a full magazine an’ I started crawlin’ on my belly toward that machine gun nest an’ then slippin’ from tree to tree. It was mornin’ an’ there was a bit of a fog, which helped…Felt a burnin’ in my leg an’ knew I’d been hit, but figured it was a long way from my heart, an’ I managed to get close enough to that German emplacement I could see the crew shootin’ at us.”

Joe and John paddled around another hundred yards or so past the Cobb still, checking the creek for any sign of Ellie Hargrave’s body.

Joe was in the bow, sculling the craft forward while John steered side to side from the stern looking under some of the roots that extended to the creek from the big trees along the bank.

"Be lucky if we find her, John."

"I know, but we have to try. This creek is the only lead we have to those girls…I'm afraid we may not find her, but then again, guess I'm more afraid we will."

"How much further upstream do you want to go?"

"At least another hundred yards or so, then we'll head back downstream."

"That when you found that pistol?" I asked.

"Nope. It was after I managed to drop the officer headin' up the crew…Wellsir, they stopped shootin' for a couple of seconds…long enough for me to dive into their trench an' was lucky enough to take 'em all out…I waved at my unit that had been pinned down an' they over ran the rest of the German troops in that sector."

Hutch was gettin' excited at the story. "Is that when ya'll won the battle?"

He shook his head. "Not quite, but it did help a little…I crawled over to that dead officer and he had this gun in his hand." He patted the holster on his hip. "Didn't figure he needed it anymore so I...uh, confiscated it. That's the last thing I remembered till I woke up in the hospital...They said I had passed out from losin' blood from my wound."

"Gol-uh-olee." Hutch's eyes were big as saucers.

Joe sculled the nose around toward the opposite bank.

"Hold it, Joe." John backwatered a little.

"What is it?"

"Thought I saw something move through the trees yonder." He pointed. "Pull into the bank.

"What do you think it was?"

"Swear it was a flash of yellow."

Joe sculled over to the edge, stepped out in the water and pulled the bow up on the bank. John walked forward and stepped out beside him.

"Over that way."

"Listen, John, hear that?"

"Something's movin' on the other side of that copse of dogwood...You go that way, I'll go this...Oh, my God!"

They both could see a figure staggering through the woods, it fell, got back up and grabbed hold of one of the dogwood saplings.

Joe and John charged through the woods to the side of a young girl in a torn and tattered yellow dress—it was Ellie Hargrave.

She collapsed to the forest floor as they arrived.

"My God, John, she's alive."

"This girl's been through hell."

John bent over, picked her up, cradling her limp, emaciated form like a baby. Joe led the way back to the boat, pushing branches out of the way for John.

He climbed in the boat and sat down on the rear seat holding the unconscious Ellie to his chest. "Let's get back to the truck. Gotta get this girl to the hospital."

Joe paddled the boat back to the swimming hole and bumped into the bank. Tom jumped up and pulled the bow up so Joe could help pull it further out of the water.

John clambered out and rushed up the slope to the truck.

"Is that her, Daddy?"

"Yeah, Foot."

"She still alive?" asked Hutch.

Daddy nodded.

Tom rushed past grandpa to open the door for him. He took Ellie's limp form from him so he could get in, then he handed her back. She looked like a rag doll.

"Ya'll get on the back, got to get her to town."

"Joe, she's really dehydrated, need to get some water in her first…might not make it to town. Could tell when I took her from John."

"Good idea, Tom, let's go to the house, Joe. See as Mame can get some water in her."

Daddy jumped in the driver's side an' started the truck up while me, Hutch, an' Tom piled on the bed.

He backed around an' headed to the road. Good thing the Haynesville Road was oiled. Fast as daddy drove, we'd a been covered in dust. Had to hang on tight when he turned down grandpa's road an' slid to a stop at the house.

Grandpa didn't run, but he walked real fast up the flagstone walkway yellin' for grandma all the way.

"Mame! Mame!"

Grandma an' mama both come out the screendoor. She was dryin' her hands on a dishtowel.

"What in landsakes, John…Oh, my Lord, get that girl inside, put her on our bed. Vertis, bring a pan of water."

Mama turned an' headed back down toward the kitchen.

"She's really dehydrated, Mame, need to get some inside her, too," said Tom.

"I'll help, grandma." I took off after mama to get a glass.

Grandpa took her on in their bedroom an' laid her on the bed. I beat mama back with the glass of water as she couldn't run with that pan. I handed it to grandma.

"Prop her up, John."

Ellie's eyes kinda fluttered, opened an' had a kinda wild look in 'em, like she was scared plumb to death.

Grandma held the glass to her lips. “Here, honey, drink some of this.”

It was like she wadn’t sure what grandma was sayin’, but when some of the cool water touched her lips, she started to drink.

“Slow, Ellie, drink slow.”

Mama set the pan on the night stand, dipped a washrag in it, wrung it out, an’ started wipin’ her arms an’ hands which was really dirty.

Tom leaned over an’ looked real close in her face, ‘specially at her eyes.

“Mame, need to cover her up an’ get a pillow under her feet…She’s in shock.”

§§§

CHAPTER TWENTY-THREE

THREE CREEKS BOTTOM

Mason Cobb ran blindly through the dense woods away from the moonshine still area and the murderous gunfire from Big John, his son-in-law, and the World War I veteran. He'd recognized Tom Rayford when he stepped out of the woods pointing that gun at him.

The gunfire had long since ceased when he stopped, winded, and collapsed to his knees to catch his breath.

He staggered to his feet after a couple of minutes, and circled back around to spy on the still from another direction—pure, evil, hatred burned in his eyes and heart.

He mumbled as he worked his way back, "Gonna die, all of 'em gonna die…last thang I do."

Cobb peered through the foliage at the carnage of his three sons laying scattered about the clearing like shattered puppets with their strings cut in pools of their own blood—Big John, the kid, and the others were gone.

He stepped into the open area, checked each of his boys and dropped to his knees again beside his oldest, Harley. "Dead, all dead…my boys. Damn John Jamison's soul, damn it…an' all his kin an' kind, to hell."

JAMISON HOME

"Have to get her warm, Mame. Seen strong men die from shock…She's in a bad way."

Tom looked at grandpa like he was really concerned, an' I guess he was.

Grandpa looked down at her. "Mame, let's move her into the spare bedroom on that feather bed an' get a couple quilts on her…this bed's too hard for her." He turned to daddy. "Shouldn't oughta move her to town till she's better, don't you think, Joe?"

"Totally agree to that, John…Fact is, when you radio the hospital from the sheriff's car to go out an' get the bodies, why don't you see about having Doctor Duckworth come out here? He should check her over."

Tom turned to grandpa. "I can take your truck an' meet the meat wagon boys on Haynesville Road an' lead 'em down in the bottom, John. They'll never find that still otherwise."

"Believe you're right on that, Tom. Can't tell you how much I appreciate all your help."

"Don't think anything about it…Doing what has to be done."

Mama was still wipin' Ellie down with that damp rag an' cleanin' her face. She was right pretty with all the dirt gone, but she kept cuttin' her eyes 'round like she was in a cage or somethin'.

Mama held up her arm a little an' turned to grandpa. "She was tied, Daddy. Look at these marks."

Grandpa nodded. "Believe you're right, Vertis…poor baby."

Daddy stepped over to the bed. "Let's go ahead and move her across the hall to that spare bedroom, Mame…See if we can get some more water in her over there."

Grandpa turned to Tom. "Let's go outside an' radio the hospital, then you can take my truck back out yonder to meet the ambulance."

They left out the door while daddy picked Ellie up. Looked like she didn't weigh nothin'. He carried her out 'cross the big hall an' into the room next to his an' mama's.

Grandma opened her big cedar chest, grabbed a couple of quilts an' followed daddy.

I looked over at Hutch. "How 'bout us go listen to grandpa use that radio thing in the sheriff's car. Ain't never seen one of those work before."

"Me neither, let's go."

Mama stopped me with her hand on my shoulder. "You sure you boys are all right? They didn't hurt you, beside that busted lip, did they?"

"No, ma'am, we were just scared mostly."

"Well, come back inside as soon as your grandpa and Tom use that radio and I'll fix ya'll a snack till suppertime…I'm going to heat some water for a bath, too. You both need it."

"Aw, Mama."

She raised her eyebrows at me. "Foot."

Hutch was tryin' to hide behind me while mama was lookin' me over, but she got him, too.

"Yessum."

We hooked it out to the front door an' followed grandpa an' Tom to the sheriff's car.

We sat down on the ground beside the open front door of the car. Tom leaned in with his arms on the top while grandpa sat in the driver's seat an' turned the radio on.

"Hello, dispatch, this is sheriff's unit One, come back."

There was some static an' some poppin' an' a voice come out of that radio.

"This is dispatch, go ahead John…Over."

"Contact the hospital. Have them send a meat wagon out the Haynesville Road. Tom Rayford will meet them just past Three Creeks. He'll be in my truck. Will lead the boys down to where the bodies are…Over."

"How many deceased are we talkin' about, John? Over."

"Three. Another moonshine still…Over."

"Come back with that, John."

"Another moonshine still…Also contact Doctor Duckworth to come to my house…Over."

"What's the problem there?…Over."

"Tell him when he gets here. One out."

"Roger that, One. Dispatch out."

Grandpa looked up at Tom. "Figure it'll take 'em about forty-five minutes. Let's go back in an' have a cup of coffee, what say?"

Tom grinned. "Thought you'd never bring it up."

Grandpa stepped out of the car. Me an' Hutch scrambled to get out of the way of Tom steppin' back. We followed 'em back inside—we was both gettin' a little hungry.

We saw Bobby, Don, an' Hubert comin' 'round the barn from the direction of the woods 'fore we got to the door. Don was carryin' a big mess of fish on a stringer. The bottom was draggin' on the ground. Tiny was prancin' alongside like she'd helped catch 'em.

I elbowed Hutch. "Reckon we're havin' fish for supper."

"Oh, yum."

"Ya'll caught a nice mess of fish."

Bobby grinned. "Yeah, they were nearly jumpin' up on the bank tryin' to get to the stringer."

"What ya'll been doin', playin' tag or somethin'?" asked Don.

Me an' Hutch glanced at each other.

I shrugged. "Oh, nothin' much. Just havin' gunfights with moonshiners, bustin' up a still, an' rescuin' that missin' girl with grandpa, Mister Tom, an' daddy's all."

"Do what?"

"Tell you 'bout it later. Looks like ya'll got some fish to clean."

"Could use some help."

I shook my head. "Catch 'em, you gotta clean 'em, big brother."

They walked around the side of the house to the back to a old table where we cleaned fish, skinned squirrels, an' such. Knew they better not bring those fish in grandma's house before cleanin' 'em. She'd peel their heads like a onion.

A little after sundown, we was sittin' round the dinin' table finishin' off the fish. Had lots of choices, too. They had caught some flathead cats, several weighed three or four pounds, blue gill bream, an' crappie, too. Grandma fileted 'em an' fried 'em up. Melt in your mouth—uh-huh.

Also had some fried cornbread, buttered creamed corn an' fried sweet taters. Saved room for the dewberry cobbler, though.

Tom was back an' grandma made him an' Doctor Duckworth stay for supper. You don't argue with grandma.

Tom was fillin' grandpa an' everbody in on pickin' up the Cobb boys down in the bottom.

He looked to grandpa, an' then daddy. "Could tell old man Cobb had been back since we left earlier…all the guns were gone. Guess he came to check on his boys…Suspect he's going to be a bit upset…Best keep an eye out an' watch your back."

Grandpa wiped the clabber from his upper lip. "Goin' to be well-armed, then. He could get here same way Foot an' Hutch got to the creek…cross country." He looked at us. "Little over a mile wouldn't you say, boys?"

We nodded, but didn't say nothin' 'cause our mouths were full of cobbler an' whipped cream. Tiny was at my feet waitin' to lick the bowls.

Bobby, Don, an' Hubert sat there with their mouths hangin' open listenin' to all that happened. Mama told 'em that wadn't polite. Knew they'd missed out, but we wouldn't have had fish for supper, though—guess that was some consolation.

Grandma got up to go in the kitchen. "Think that bone broth is ready, Ralph. Want to go with me when I see if I can get her to eat some?"

He wiped his mouth with a linen napkin and got to his feet. "I do indeed, Mame. Right concerned with that child." He looked at grandpa. "Probably need to go get Benson and Mildred over here. I'm sure they'll feel some better that ya'll found their daughter. But I don't want her moved yet…She's just almost catatonic."

I kinda wrinkled my forehead. "What's cat-a-tonic, Doctor Duckworth?"

"It's an unresponsive state, Foot, sometimes produced by shock. Their eyes are open, but they don't seem to see anything."

"Is that for good?"

"Let's hope not. Most people come out of it…eventually. Just hope there's no other damage."

Grandma came back through carryin' a tray with a bowl of her broth an' another glass of water. "Coming, Ralph?"

"Right behind you, Mame."

Grandpa got up. "I'll run over to get the Hargraves…want a ride to your place, Tom?"

"I'd appreciate it, John. Tell Mame I really enjoyed the supper."

"I heard that, Tom, and you're welcome here anytime," came her voice from the hallway.

Me an' Hutch sat our bowls on the floor for Tiny, then followed grandma an' the doctor to Ellie's room. Wanted to understand this cat-a-tonic thing better.

We went in, grandma set the tray on the nightstand an' turned up the coal oil lamp. Ellie had quit flickin' her eyes 'round an' was just starin' at the ceilin'.

The doc pulled the covers back an' went to checkin' her with his stethoscope thing an' feelin' of her pulse. Then he held his finger in front of her eyes an' moved it back an' forth. He shook his head.

"Ellie, can you hear me?"

Her eyes moved to his face.

"Ellie, how do you feel?"

She never opened her mouth, just stared at him like she had at the ceilin'.

The doc turned to grandma an' frowned. "This is not uncommon. She can hear…but I don't think the child can speak."

§§§

CHAPTER TWENTY-FOUR

THREE CREEKS BOTTOM

Mason Cobb stalked away from the ruined still toward a makeshift cabin he and his boys had built deeper in the bottom, mumbling. He carried his son's weapons—a thirty-eight revolver, a Colt .44, and a double barreled twelve gauge shotgun, plus his own ancient .45 Remington revolver.

THREE CREEKS

The Cobb clan had built the shelter in the bottom so they wouldn't have to drive all the way to their ramshackled house close to Junction City to use while they were brewing a batch of shine.

He played a number of revenge scenarios in his head as he walked through the dense woods.

Cobb opened the handmade plank door hung with leather scraps for hinges, went inside, laid the guns on a rickety table they used to eat on and lit a coal oil lamp against the evening darkness. He threw himself down on a lice infested bunk, picked up a jug of his squeezings next to the bed on the dirt floor and unscrewed the cap.

After a long pull of the potent liquor, he set it back on the floor, grinned and nodded. "Burn 'em out. That's what I'll do. Burn 'em out…The lot of 'em. Let 'em roast in hell…Kill my boys…tear up my stills…show 'em."

He picked the jug up and took another pull.

JAMISON HOME

Grandma was able to get Ellie to take near half of the bowl of bone broth 'fore she dropped back off.

She looked at Doctor Duckworth as they walked out of the room an' closed the door behind 'em. "That should help her, plus the rest. No tellin' how long she was lost in those woods."

Me an' Hutch had hustled out when I saw her get out of the chair she was sittin' in next to the bed an' cover Ellie back up.

The doc shook his head. "Wonder how she got free?"

They walked into the kitchen where daddy, grandpa an' Tom sat at the kitchen table havin' some after dinner coffee.

Bobby, Don, an' Hubert were out on the front porch, watchin' fireflies.

Grandma shook her head. "There's no tellin'. Must have been something awful the child had been goin' through…maybe she saw who killed Bethany and Loretta."

Grandpa got to his feet. "Well, my money's on Cobb and his boys, what with the youngest sparkin' her…Don't believe in coincidences."

Daddy looked up from his cup. "He's sure at the top of the list alright."

Tom turned to him, then grandpa. "Who else is on that list?"

Grandpa shook his head. "That's the thing, Tom...don't really have a list. Guess I'll run on over, tell the Hargraves, and drop Tom off at his place."

"And we'll just have to wait and hope Ellie can eventually speak...and tell us what happened."

"Hows come she can't talk, Doctor Duckworth?"

He looked down at me. "Well, Foot, it's called Aphasia. That's just a fancy medical name for being emotionally overcome by some sort of trauma or circumstances. It's her mind's way of dealing with the experience to protect itself...for now. Understand?"

I looked at Hutch, an' then back at the doc an' shook my head. "Uh-uh." I cocked my head as I thought on what he said for a second. "Does it mean she's just kinda hidin' from everthing?"

He smiled. "Couldn't have said it better myself, Foot. Have to remember that..." The doc glanced at grandpa. "From the mouths of babes..."

"How's Myron doing?"

"Ornery as ever, John...Oh, get a chance, might want to come in and freshen up his flask...seems at least to help his disposition."

"Found it, huh?"

The doc nodded. "Had a taste myself. Not bad. Think I got a whiff of watermelon in it."

Grandpa grinned. "Thought so myself."

"John L. Franklin Jamison!"

"Just tasted it to make sure it was all right, Mame…No tellin' what some of the moonshine out there has in it."

Grandma crossed her arms an' tapped her foot. "Uh-huh."

Grandpa just looked at the floor, then turned to Tom. "Ready?"

"When you are."

Think grandpa just wanted to get out from underneath grandma's stare.

Daddy an' mama looked at each other an' grinned. Believe they'd seen it before…To be so little an' skinny, grandma don't cut much slack to anybody.

"Tell the Hargraves they should wait till in the mornin' to come see Ellie, John. She needs all the rest she can get. I'll be back out in the morning, too."

"I'll have you some breakfast ready, Ralph."

He stepped over an' gave grandma a peck on the cheek. "Thanks, Mame, you're one of a kind."

She got this kinda almost grin. "I know…Now get out of here…and John, tell Matilda to bring a sleeping gown for Ellie in the morning. That dress she had on may not be worth keeping, but I'll have Mamie wash it."

"Yessum." He turned an' headed down the dog run to the front door.

Grandpa an' Tom were on his heels.

"I'm gonna run home, too. Sure 'preciate the supper Miz Jamison, it was good."

"Tell Mamie I've got some linens and other things to wash tomorrow, Hutch."

"Yessum, I'll tell her."

"See you tomorrow, Hutch."

He waved over his shoulder at me as he headed to the back door. "Okay."

Daddy turned to me an' reached in his back pocket. "Picked up ya'll's sling shots." He laid both of them on the table. "Hutch can get his tomorrow."

"Thanks, Daddy, gotta learn to carry more rocks…You know what Hutch calls 'em?"

He nodded. "I know."

I grinned at him. "Just checkin'."

Grandma sat down at the table, looked like she'd had a long day, too. "I understand the services for Bethany and Loretta will be Tuesday at Jolley's Chapel."

Mama nodded. "Hope daddy'll have some answers for the families by then."

Daddy shook his head. "Wouldn't count on it, hon…unless the Hargrave girl comes around and can tell us something."

The radio crackled in the sheriff's car as John drove up to Tom's place next to Jolley's Chapel Cemetery.

"One, this is dispatch, come back."

John picked the mike up from its hook. "This is John, go ahead dispatch…Over."

"John, got a call from a couple of fishermen over near New Hope. They found a body of a teenage girl in Jordan Branch…Over."

John cut his eyes to Tom. "Copy that, dispatch. Got an exact location?…Over."

"Roger that. The conjunction of Jordan Branch with Cornie Bayou. They'll meet you at Jolley's Store…Over."

"Roger, dispatch. Less than a quarter mile from there. On my way…Contact Doctor Duckworth and the hospital. Meet us there…One out."

"Roger that, One…Dispatch out."

John looked at Tom again. "Still want me to drop you at your place?"

Tom cocked an eyebrow at him.

John nodded. "Yeah." He turned the Ford around and drove up to Jolley's Store.

Two men walked down the stoop and up to the car.

"Hidy, John."

"Charlie…Eli. Ya'll know Tom, don'tcha?"

They both leaned over to look through the window.

"You bet, how you doin', Tom?"

He shook his head. "Fair to partly cloudy, Eli."

"What did you boys find?"

They exchanged glances.

"Found the Riley girl, John…drowned, I guess," commented Charlie. "This makes three, don't it?"

John took a deep breath. "Yeah…Got to wait for Doc Duckworth and the ambulance from the hospital to get here, then we'll follow you. That alright?"

"Shore, just get us a soda water. Ya'll want one?"

John glanced over at Tom who shook his head.

"Pass, Charlie, just had supper, but thanks."

Charlie and Eli stepped back up on the porch. Charlie put a nickel in the slot on the Nehi box by the door, opened the lid, and Eli pulled out a Nehi orange. He put another nickel in and got a RC cola for himself.

They popped them on the opener on the side, the lids dropping down in the bin below.

Eli took a drink of his orange soda. "Smead's gonna have to empty the lid catcher. Gittin' purty full."

"Say, Charlie, how'd ya'll leave the body?"

He turned around to the sheriff's car. "Uh…tied her wrist to a root, John…Keep her from floatin' off. Didn't figure we oughta touch her more'n that…Seen some of them Bogie cop movies."

John rolled his eyes while Tom shook his head. They looked up as headlights pulled in from the road. An ambulance, its lights flashing, came in right behind Doctor Duckworth.

John got out and walked over to the Buick. "Made good time, doc…"

"Saw the ambulance comin' with its lights on I waved 'em down…they told me. I turned around. Know who it is?"

John nodded. "The Riley girl."

"Oh, damn, another teenager. Well, ya'll lead the way."

John circled his hand over his head at Charlie and Eli to indicate 'let's go'. They nodded, got in Eli's Chevy pickup and pulled out on the Haynesville Road—John and the others followed.

Eli turned down a dirt road that led to the confluence of Jordan Branch with Cornie Bayou. It was only two hundred yards or so.

John grabbed the flashlight from the glove box and stepped out.

Charlie and Eli led the way down to the bank of Jordan Branch. Charlie carried a coal oil lantern. He held it high over his head.

The light reflected off the pale skin of young Jennifer Riley. The dark-haired girl was wearing a blue gingham summer dress and was barefoot.

John untied the cotton fish stringer from around her wrist. He and Tom lifted her on out of the water and placed her on the stretcher the medics had laid on the bank.

Doctor Duckworth knelt down. “Shine your light here, John.”

He panned the long flashlight over to her face, the eyes were open and glassy. The doctor turned her head a little to each side, and then looked up at John and grimaced. “Same MO, strangled an’ neck broken…Know about the rest when I do the autopsy.”

§§§

CHAPTER TWENTY-FIVE

EL DORADO MEMORIAL HOSPITAL

John walked into Sheriff Wilson's room as the early morning sun was streaming through the east side window.

The head of the sheriff's bed was raised and he had a tray across his lap with a bowl of oatmeal, a plate of dry toast, and a cup of coffee. He looked up after tasting his breakfast and frowned.

John grinned. "Well, Myron, you don't look much better."

"Not surprised." He pointed to the bowl. "See what they give me to eat…cold oatmeal an' no butter or sugar…gag."

"Think you'd complain if you were hung with a new rope…Bring you some of Mame's biscuits an' sausage next time."

"Coulda brought it this time."

"Coulda, but brought this instead." He held up a pint Mason jar of clear liquid. "Doc said to freshen up your flask."

"Well, bless his little black heart…Just leave the whole jar, you don't mind."

"Figured that's what you'd say."

"What's been happenin'?"

"One reason why I'm here. You're not goin' to like it."

The sheriff rolled his eyes. "Alright let's have it."

John pulled up a slat-backed wooden chair, the only one in the room. He turned it backward, straddled it and sat down next to the bed.

Thirty minutes later, John finished telling about the run in with the Cobbs, the kidnapping of Foot and Hutch, and the subsequent shoot out and killing of the three Cobb boys."

"I'God, John…Nothin' happens around here for a year, then all hell starts breakin' loose…"

"Well, that's not all, Myron."

"There's more?"

John nodded. "Found another body."

The sheriff set up. "What?" He squinted his eyes. "Don't tell me…"

"Yep, afraid so."

"Are you goin' to tell me about it or just keep me in suspense all mornin'?"

"Was gettin' to it…We pulled the Riley girl out of Jordan Branch near Cornie Bayou…"

Doctor Duckworth walked in the room. "Figured you'd be here John. Guess he told you, Myron…"

"And I guess you're going to give me the details."

The doctor nodded. "Did the autopsy last night. It's the chain killer all right. Strangled…same bruising on the neck, neck broken at the third cervical, an' like the other two…pregnant."

The sheriff set his tray on the night stand and started to throw back the covers. "I gotta get outta here…"

"The hell you are." Doctor Duckworth pushed him back down. "You tear those stitches to your artery and you'll bleed to death before they can get you back to the hospital."

He frowned. "How long?"

"How long, what?"

"Before I can get out of this asylum."

"Minimum of two more weeks…Not open to discussion."

"Son of a…"

"This isn't a new case, Myron…The Riley girl had been dead about the same length of time as the others." The doctor turned to John. "You tell him about finding Ellie Hargrave?"

John shook his head. "Hadn't gotten that far."

"Not dead?"

Duckworth shook his head and looked at John.

"Joe an' I found her staggerin' through the woods down near Three Creeks. Her hands had been tied, but she got loose, somehow."

"What'd she say?"

John frowned. "Nothin'…yet."

"What the hell do you mean, 'nothing, yet'."

It was John's turn to look at the doctor to talk.

"She's still in shock, Myron, she won't talk…or can't."

The sheriff frowned at Doctor Duckworth. "You are going to tell me why, aren't you?"

"She's got what's called trauma induced aphasia…"

"Meanin' she's still too scared to talk?"

"That's pretty much it, Myron."

John turned to look at the sheriff. "Tom mentioned to me he'd seen the same thing from men in combat…What we do know is, all the girls are about the same age an' from the same school in Junction City." He glanced at the doctor. "All murdered the same way…found in water, clothed, but barefoot…all pregnant. We don't know about Ellie Hargrave…being pregnant or not that is…but she's the only one still wearin' shoes."

"And they were all friends?"

John nodded. "That's my understandin'."

"Suspects?"

He held up one big finger. “Cobb…The youngest was seein’ Ellie…Only thing is, when we busted that first still, I checked around for footprints after they hauled you off.”

“And?”

“Found a girl’s barefoot print ‘longside a man wearing brogans down at the creek bank.”

“Didn’t you say the Hargrave girl was wearin’ shoes?”

John nodded. “Black and white saddle oxfords…and all the Cobbs were wearin’ boots.”

Sheriff Wilson puffed up his cheeks and blew his breath out.

The doctor’s eyes twinkled. “As Sherlock Holmes said, ‘There is nothing more deceptive than an obvious fact.’.”

JAMISON HOME

Hutch walked up red hill road from his grandmother’s house with her. Mamie was coming up to do the Jamison’s wash.

He ran on ahead when they got close as he knew she would be going around to the back to start the fire under the wash pot.

A pair of bloodshot brown eyes watched the pair from a copse of persimmon trees on the other side of John's truck garden.

Those eyes burned with the unquenchable fires of hate as John Jamison pulled up in front of the house in Sheriff Wilson's car followed by Doctor Duckworth's Buick.

The men got out, both walked up the flagstones to the front porch and entered the big house. The doctor carried his black bag.

I looked up as Hutch ran into the kitchen where I was sittin' at the table.

"Hey, Foot."

"Hey, Hutch."

"Whatcha doin'?"

"Was gonna help grandma shell some peas...wanna help?"

"Sure, I'm about the best pea sheller there is."

"Are not,"

"Am too."

"Are not."

"Am too...We'll have a contest."

"Deal…Oh, here's your sling shot."

"My what?" He looked down as I pushed his over toward him. "Daddy picked 'em both up yesterday for us down to Three Creeks."

"Why'd you call it a sling shot?"

"'Cause that's what daddy calls 'em…that or a wrist rocket." I raised my eyebrows an' shrugged.

"He don't call 'em a…"

"Uh-uh…Says that ain't polite."

"Really?…Huh, didn't know that. Who decides that stuff?"

"Beats me. Somebody smarter'n us, I guess."

"Whatever."

Grandma handed us each a bowl an' a paper sack of purple hull crowders.

"You boys take these out on the porch to shell them. Vertis and I will join ya'll in a bit. Got to get the laundry ready for Mamie."

Grandma looked up as grandpa an' Doctor Duckworth came in the kitchen.

"Mornin' Mame, got any breakfast left?"

"Thought you'd be here earlier, Ralph."

He looked at grandpa. "Well, John showed up an' we had to bring Myron up to snuff. Had to threaten to tie him in the bed when we left."

"Gettin' cabin fever already?"

"Could say so."

Grandma smiled. "Got some biscuits left an' I'll warm up the gravy after you take a look at Ellie...Her folks got here right after John left for town...Brought a sleepin' gown and a clean dress."

"Did she respond to them?"

Grandma looked at the doctor, mashed her lips together an' shook her head. "Nothin'. I even let Mildred feed her some Creme of Wheat. She ate, but not a lot."

"Any kind of activity is good."

"I cautioned them not to show too much emotion while they were in there like you suggested last night if Ellie didn't respond to them."

"Did they?"

"No, but they both cried after they came out an' we went to the kitchen. I told them to thank the Lord that at least she didn't wind up like the other girls...Seemed to help some."

Grandma looked at me an' Hutch. "You boys get on out to the porch an' get started on those peas...Now, scat."

"Come on, Hutch, 'fore grandma starts workin' us over with that dish towel."

"Right behind you…Still gonna win."

"Are not."

"Are too."

They continued arguing all the way down the dog run to the front door.

Doctor Duckworth grinned an' shook his head. "Those boys really like each other don't they?"

"They do. It's nice to see, too."

She followed him down the hall to Ellie Hargrave's room and brought a cool glass of water for her. John followed along behind them, but stopped at the door and just peeked in to watch.

Doctor Duckworth set his bag on the night stand, opened it and removed his stethoscope.

"Good morning, Ellie. Can you hear me?"

Her eyes cut toward him. There was only the slightest nod.

"How do you feel?"

There was no response…

§§§

CHAPTER TWENTY-SIX

JAMISON HOME

"I got more'n you."

I shook my head. "Uh-uh."

Hutch tilted his bowl toward me. "See."

"Look 'bout the same to me."

"You're just lookin' at 'em crooked."

"'Cause you're holdin' your bowl crooked…Look at all the hulls you got in yours. They go in the bucket for Sally an' Ted."

There was a quarter bushel bucket sittin' 'tween us.

"Ted?"

"Grandpa's Tennessee plowin' mule…Him an' Sally like 'em when they're fresh."

"Well, even if I takn' 'em out, still got more'n you."

Tiny was laying on the porch in front of my feet. Her head was turnin' back an' forth lookin' at whoever was talkin'.

"Do not."

"Do…"

Hutch was interrupted by the screen door opening behind us. We turned to see Ellie, standin' there in her white sleepin' gown. She was lookin' 'round like she was lost or somethin'.

"Ellie, are you okay?"

Grandma had brushed her red hair till it shined like she did hers, an' she turned the purtyest green eyes I ever seen to me.

There was a tear formin' in one an' it started rollin' down her cheek. The way the light hit, it looked like a diamond.

I didn't know what to do, but she looked like she oughta be hugged. So I got up an' hugged her. She was a little taller'n me, but that didn't matter none.

Then more tears came, 'cause I could feel 'em drippin' on my face. I started cryin', too, but I don't know why.

"Go get grandma. Go get grandma."

Hutch jumped up, ran through the door an' down to the kitchen.

In a minute, he came back with grandma an' mama. I looked up at her.

"She came out the door, Grandma, an' started…started cryin'." I shook my head. "Didn't know…what…what to do but hug her…It made me cry…cry, too." I sniffed 'cause my nose started runnin'.

Grandpa, Doctor Duckworth, an' Daddy came out the screen door, too, guess they'd been havin' another cup of coffee.

I noticed mama was cryin' an' Grandma's eyes teared up, too.

"Oh, child. You did just the right thing. She just needed to be loved. Here, I'll take over. Blow your nose an' wipe your eyes." She handed me her dish towel an' wrapped her arms around Ellie. "Let it go, child, let it go. You're safe now."

I blew my nose an' looked at Hutch an' danged if he was cryin', too. I handed him the dish towel so he could blow his nose.

Grandma looked over at me. "Did she say anything?"

"Uh-uh." Shook my head a couple times. "Just started cryin' when she looked at me an' Hutch."

The bloodshot brown eyes of Mason Cobb watched the activity on the porch from the copse of persimmon trees on the other side of the truck garden. He spat a stream of noxious tobacco juice to the side and wiped his chin with his sleeve.

He sneered and nodded. "Come back tonight."

Doctor Duckworth touched grandma on the shoulder. "Set her down in that rocker when you feel it’s right, Mame. I’m going to get my stethoscope.”

She nodded at him before he turned an’ went back in the house.

Grandma continued huggin’ Ellie an’ it seemed to relax her some.

Mama leaned over to grandma. “I’ll go get her a glass of water.”

Daddy an’ grandpa just stood there, not sure of what to do, but watch.

The doc came back out with his stethoscope thing an’ waited till grandma guided Ellie to the rockin’ chair I’d been sittin’ in.

He put the end things in his ears an’ the other end that was ‘bout the size of a half-dollar an’ shiny, on her chest in several places. Then he held her wrist an’ looked at his watch. Not sure why ‘less he had to be somewhere.

“Her pulse is now pretty normal and so is her respiration.” He looked at grandma. “Think you can put that dress on her and let her sit out on the porch a while. Don’t want her goin’ home yet…know how Benson and Mildred would be around her.”

Grandma an’ mama exchanged glances.

“We’ll keep an eye on her.”

“Knew you would. Well, I have to get back to town, got other patients to see.”

“Let me put together a little care package for Myron. Might help his attitude some.”

The doctor grinned. “Can’t hurt any…”

“Make one for you, too.”

“Was hopin’ you’d say that.”

“Known you a long time, Ralph.” She grabbed her dish towel back from me an’ swatted him with it before she turned to go in the house.

“Vertis, take Ellie back inside an’ put that pretty little dress her mama brought on her and brush her hair out again. Having brushed hair will make her feel better…does me.” She kept the screen door from slammin’ shut behind her.

Mama got Ellie up an’ took her back inside. Me an’ Hutch went to shellin’ peas again.

Daddy an’ grandpa looked around, then at each other.

“Guess I’ll go to the garden an’ get Mame some fresh tomatoes, okra, an’ squash she wanted for supper to go with the pork chops…comin’, Joe?”

Hutch an’ me looked at each other an’ we both went, “Yum.”

“Right with you, John.”

Joe and John moved down the path between a row of tomatoes and a row of okra. Joe was picking the ripe tomatoes and John was cutting the okra that was ready with his Boker three bladed pocket knife. Joe carried the bucket both used.

"Think we need to see if we can chase down Cobb?"

John pitched an okra pod into the bucket. "Ought to. Be like huntin' a needle in a haystack down there in that bottom, though."

"Reckon he might come to us?...Never seen such hate in a man's eyes before."

"That's been my thoughts, Joe. Kinda dangerous. Might be putting the family at risk is what bothers me."

"Any ideas?"

"One, let's always have our guns in our pockets...anywhere we are. 'Specially around the house here."

Joe patted his rear pocket. "Thought of that already."

John grinned and nodded. "Yeah, me too."

Me, Hutch, mama, grandma, an' Ellie all sat on the porch shellin' peas, 'cept for Ellie—she just watched. We looked over as she bent down, picked up Tiny, set her in her lap an' started pettin' her.

Grandma nodded an' grabbed another handful of peas from the sack, put 'em in her bowl to shell. Think she was pleased with what she saw.

Ellie smiled as Tiny ate up the attention an' gave her a kiss.

I turned to Ellie. "Her name's Tiny. Had her since I was six. Somebody threw her out when she was a little puppy in Sulfur, Oklahoma, where we lived at the time."

She smiled again an' hugged Tiny. Got another kiss for it.

Grandma got to her feet an' shook the paper sack into the bucket for Sally an' Ted. There was just some broke pieces left.

"You boys hand me your bowls."

We did an' she looked at both of 'em, then at us. "Well, I have to say the winner is…" She turned to mama. "Drum roll, please."

Mama drummed her fingers real fast like a runnin' horse on the arms of her rocker.

"...the winner is...a tie. Can't see any difference at all."

She emptied our bowls into hers. "Need to go get these on for supper. Put by the rest for next winter."

I stuck my tongue out at Hutch. "See, smarty, you ain't the best there is."

"Well, neither are you."

"Didn't say I was, just said you wadn't...so there."

Ellie looked at me an' Hutch, then at grandma—she almost giggled.

After supper an' fresh peach cobbler, we took our tea goblets an' got up from the bench. Ellie ate at the table with us, but still didn't say nothin'.

"Mama, Hutch wants to spend the night an' would it be awright we sleep on the screened-in back porch?...Ain't room in me an' Bobby's bed, 'sides he kicks."

"'Cause you flop around all night."

"Do not."

"How do you know?"

"Well…Just do, that's all." I looked back at mama. "Can we?"

She looked at grandma who nodded.

"I'll make them up some pallets. Be cooler out there anyway."

"Thanks, Grandma."

She looked at Ellie. "Are you ready for bed, honey?"

Ellie nodded an' got up from the table an' hugged grandma.

After she went to bed, me an' Hutch sat out on the front porch while grandma an' mama made us up a couple of pallets right next to the back screen door where we could see the stars to the east an' the half-moon that would be up in a little bit.

Grandma stepped out the front door. "Pallets are ready, boys, anytime ya'll are ready to turn in."

I looked at Hutch an' we both nodded, hugged grandma, mama, daddy, an' grandpa, an' headed down the dog run to the back porch.

Wadn't long 'fore everbody else went to their beds—been a long day.

Several hours later, all the lamps in the house were down to their overnight setting. The half-moon was up—all was quiet.

A dark shadow carrying a glass jug ran across the road from the red hill and up to the side of the house.

The figure knelt down, wadded up several sheets of newspaper and stuffed them underneath the house which was up on stacks of rocks a little over a foot high. He unscrewed the lid, poured most of the liquid from the glass container over the newspaper, set the jug back down, reached in the pocket of his overalls and removed a battered Zippo lighter. Light from the half-moon glinted off the top as the man flipped it open and rolled his thumb over the striker wheel…

§§§

CHAPTER TWENTY-SEVEN

JAMISON HOME

“You know, you never told me your real name.”

Hutch looked out the screen that started ‘bout four feet from the floor an’ went to the ceilin’ at the half-moon that was just above the tree line in the sky to the east of the house.

"Seymour Washington Grant...Daddy's family took the name of Grant for the general what led the war against the south when they was freed."

"Seymour? See why your mama called you Hutch."

"What's yours?"

"Henry Lightfoot Lee...I tol' you 'bout my daddy's ancestors, a Henry 'Lighthorse Harry' Lee, from the Revolution against England, an' Francis Lightfoot Lee. He signed the Declaration 'long with some other fellas...Robert E. Lee's my third great uncle or somethin' like that."

"I like just plain Foot better...General Grant an' General Lee fought against each other durin' the war that freed us coloreds, didn't they?"

"What I heard...Glad we don't fight."

Couldn't see in what little light that was comin' from the moon, but knew he was noddin' his head.

"How's come you got all those freckles?"

"I don't know...Daddy used to say that when I was little, I walked up behind a cow that was eatin' bran an' she farted."

Thought Hutch was goin' to choke to death, gigglin'.

Tiny was layin' 'tween us an' suddenly raised her head an' looked toward the screen. She had a kinda low growl in her throat.

Hutch nudged me. "What's that?"

I listened a minute. "Probably just a coon 'er a possum rustlin' 'round."

"Tiny don't like it."

She got to her feet an' trotted over to the screen door an' put her nose 'tween the edge an' the jamb an' pushed…

"For Algernon, Harley, Jase, an' Berty…" Cobb rolled his thumb over the striker wheel again, some sparks flew, but no flame. He did it once more. The sparks lit the wick and a weak yellow flame sprung up.

Me an' Hutch sat bolt upright as Tiny pushed the screen door open an' ran outside, barkin' real fast an' loud like terriers do…Rar-rar-rar-rar-rar.

A man screamed from outside as Tiny's bark turned to a growlin' snarl like she was chewin' on somethin.

We jumped up as a light came out of mama an' daddy's room like they turned up the coal oil lantern. I could see daddy charge out the door in just his khaki pants.

Me an' Hutch was only wearin' our underwear, but we ran outside anyway to see a dark figure runnin' in the moonlight toward the red hill road with Tiny right on his heels, bitin' at his legs. We started chasin' 'em—probably a dumb thing to do, but we did it anyway.

Heard the screen door behind us slam twice. Didn't know it was daddy an' Ellie at the time.

Hutch was a bunch faster'n me an' he was catchin' up to 'em when the figure kicked at Tiny. She yelped, went rollin' off to the side of the road an' lay still.

Hutch tried to grab the guy, but he turned, hit him really hard upside the head with his fist knockin' him to the ground—he didn't move neither.

"Hutch!"

I was runnin' up to him when daddy blew past me like I was standin' still. Shoulda figured he could run 'cause mama tol' me he'd been offered a scholarship to play football at Baylor University. He couldn't take it on 'count he was the oldest boy an' his daddy, my other grandpa, had got murdered when daddy was my age. He had to work to help support the family—he had two brothers an' three sisters, but that's another story.

Daddy drove his shoulder into the man's back runnin' full speed. Musta knocked him ten or twelve feet where he skidded on his face in the middle of the red hill road.

I slid to my knees beside Hutch who still wadn't movin'. I grabbed him up an' hugged him to my chest. He was limp as a dishrag. "Hutch! Hutch! Don't you die on me! Don't you do it." I was screamin' at him through the tears rollin' down my face—he's my best friend. "Please, Hutch, be awright."

I looked up at the kajillions of stars an' the moon overhead hopin' I could see God. "Please don't let him die…please make him be okay…Please."

Back behind me, Ellie was on her knees holdin' Tiny who was whinin' an' lickin' her face at the same time an' I could see grandpa lumberin' down the hill with a big flashlight—wadn't runnin', just walkin' fast. He was just wearin' his overalls with only one strap fastened an' was barefoot, like daddy.

Could see in the pale light, the man rolled over in the dirt an' pointed a gun at daddy. The whole night lit up for a second an' there was a loud explosion that made my ears ring.

When I opened my eyes, daddy was on his knees with his .45 pointed at the man on the ground a few feet in front of him—think the guy was dead. He wadn't fast enough.

I looked down at Hutch still in my arms. His eyes fluttered an' opened.

"Would you not squeeze me so hard, Foot."

"You're alive!"

He frowned. "Well, yeah."

"You okay?"

"No…My head hurts."

Grandpa stopped beside me an' shined that big flashlight down on me an' Hutch.

Grandma an' mama were right behind him. Bobby came draggin' up the rear. He was always slow to wake up.

"You boys, alright?"

"Hutch got knocked out, but he come to…got a headache."

Mama knelt down beside us. "What in the world were ya'll doin' chasin' that man?"

"Seemed like the thing to do at the time, Mama…Tiny was after him. He was doin' somethin' next to the house…Figured it wadn't good."

I looked back at Ellie holdin' her. Her long red hair was in a single thick braid like grandma done her's at night—it was draped over her shoulder. "Is Tiny awright?…He kicked her."

Mama glanced at them. "I think so, she's licking Ellie's face."

Grandpa went on down where daddy was gettin' to his feet, still holdin' his gun. He shined the light in old man Cobb's skinned up face. His eyes was open an' he was starin' up at the sky like he was lookin' for somethin', but he wadn't seein' nothin'. There was a red stain in the middle of his chest that was gettin' bigger.

"Well, that's that. Figured might end this way." He looked at daddy. "Maybe we got our killer, too."

Daddy looked down at the moonshiner. "Sure can't get any information out of him, now…Guess we'll still have to wait on Ellie."

"I'll bring the truck down, we'll load him on the back. Not about to put that stinkin' mess in the sheriff's car. Myron'd kill me."

"Know what he was doin' up at the house?"

Grandpa shook his head. "Nope, best go check…Just leave the trash here in the road, for now. Don't think there'll be anybody come by tonight…Fact is, now that I think on it, I'll just leave 'im here an' let the morgue boys pick 'im up."

They walked back up to me an' Hutch. Mama had already got us to our feet. I put Hutch's arm across my shoulder so I could help him back up the road to the house.

Grandma got Ellie up, too. She was still holdin' Tiny, looked like her leg was hurt some, the way she held it.

"Is she awright, Ellie?"

She nodded, kissed her head an' got a kiss in return.

I looked around at everbody as we walked back up red hill road. We were all barefoot, even grandma—thought it was kinda funny.

We went to the back door of the house so we could see what daddy Cobb had been doin'.

Grandpa shined his flashlight along the side near the screen door an' back stoop. He stopped it on the jug layin' on its side in the dirt, an' then the wadded up newspaper. He picked up a cigarette lighter that was next to the jug. The lid was still open.

Daddy gathered up the wadded up newspaper under the edge of the house an' sniffed. He looked at grandpa an' raised his eyebrows. "Soaked in shine."

Grandpa whistled. "If Tiny hadn't stopped him before he got it lit…He shook his head. "…don't think any of us would be standing here right now."

He reached over to Tiny in Ellie's arms an' scratched her ears. She licked his hand.

I leaned into her an' gave her a kiss on the top of her head. "You're a hero, Tiny. A real hero."

I got a kiss back an' so did Ellie.

Grandma looked around at everone. "Anybody feel like goin' back to sleep?"

We all stared wide-eyed at her, 'cept Bobby. He said he was goin' back to bed.

"Didn't think so. Well, let's go inside and I'll make us some hot milk. How would that be?"

Me an' Hutch nudged each other as we all followed grandma inside an' sat down 'round the big kitchen table.

"I'm goin' back outside to the sheriff's car while the milk's heatin' and radio this in. Have the morgue boys at the hospital come on out an' get the body…be back in a minute."

Mama helped grandma pour up the milk in a pan an' add a few teaspoons of sugar an' a couple capfuls of vanilla flavorin'—that was my favorite part.

There were still some coals in the stove an' daddy added a few sticks of firewood from the box to get a blaze goin'.

In just a bit, it was ready. Grandpa had made it back in, too.

Mama set some big white ceramic mugs in front of everbody while the milk was heatin'. Grandma filled the cups purtnear full, an' then set down herself.

I watched as Ellie, who still held Tiny in her lap, took a sip. Her green eyes went real big an' she looked at grandma an' smiled.

Grandpa glanced across the table at her. “Ellie, did you know the man outside? Had you ever seen him before?”

She looked up at grandpa an’ just shook her head.

Daddy an’ him exchanged looks.

Grandpa took a sip of his hot milk. “Well, Joe, looks like we’re back to square one.”

§§§

CHAPTER TWENTY-EIGHT

EL DORADO MEMORIAL HOSPITAL

John tapped on the door and walked in. The sheriff raised up and blinked his eyes.

"What now?…Haven't even had my coffee yet."

John turned the chair around, straddled it, and sat down beside the sheriff's bed.

“Cobb tried to set fire to my house last night with all of us in it…Joe had to kill him. The morgue boys came got his body about two this mornin’.”

“Good God amighty…Think he was our killer?”

John stared at him for a moment, then slowly shook his head. “Ellie didn’t recognize him…Guess she never even saw him when Algernon was sparkin’ her…Can’t say as I blame the kid much. Wouldn’t take any girl I was seein’ to meet him if the old scoundrel was my father either…Had all the class of a two day old dead hog in the hot sunshine, not to say anything about being ugly as a burnt boot.”

“So now what?”

Doctor Duckworth entered the room followed by a nurse with a breakfast tray.

“Oh, God help me, runny oatmeal again…an’ cold, weak coffee.” He looked at the doctor as the nurse set his tray in his lap. “You’re doin’ this on purpose, aren’t you?”

“Now why would you say that, you old fart?”

"Because of that time I put limburger cheese on the manifold of your Model A before your date with Margie Norris in high school."

John chuckled. "You did what?"

Ralph shrugged. "You ever smelled limburger cheese burning on an exhaust manifold from the inside of a vehicle. She would never go out with me again…Took months for the stink to go away."

"You should thank me, you damned quack. Have you seen her in the last few years?…She's bigger'n John."

Duckworth grinned. "May have a point."

"I'll run over to May's in a minute…get you some of her pancakes and fried ham."

Myron nodded. "Can't wait, John. Love May's pancakes."

"Just wanted to give you an update. Least we've shut down two moonshine operations permanently…in the last week."

"Well, one consolation, the county won't have to pay for the trial…Can't say as I'll miss the Cobbs much…Did make good shine, though."

"Saved a few gallon jugs for evidence, you know."

“Don’t think I ever tasted watermelon flavored moonshine before…not bad,” commented Doctor Duckworth.

The sheriff looked up and grinned. “Yeah…Now to find that killer before he strikes again.” The sheriff looked at the doctor, and then John. “You know he won’t stop, don’t you?”

“Believe you’re right.”

“How’s Ellie?”

John turned to Duckworth. “Well, that’s the good part, Doc. She’s up and about. Ate with us last night…”

“But, still not talking?”

“Well, like I was telling Myron before you came in, she did shake her head when I asked her if she had ever seen Mason Cobb before.”

“Huh…that’s progress…I’m guessing when she does finally talk, it will come all of a sudden…like a dam breakin’. Probably needs to be around plenty of people she knows. Could spark something.”

John nodded. “Just hope it comes sooner than later. Tell her mama and daddy to take her to the funerals today.”

THREE CREEKS

JAMISON HOME

"What time are the services, Mama?" My mom turned from mixing the buttermilk an' eggs into the cornmeal to grandma.

"One o'clock. We should be finished with the food for everyone afterward well before then. Most of the other ladies will be bringing dishes, too." Grandma was stirin' a big mess of crowder peas with salt pork—part of what we shelled yesterday.

Me, Hutch, Ellie, an' Bobby was gettin' sandwiches grandma said would hold us to after the funerals for Bethany and Loretta. She called it 'brunch'. Said that's a mixin' of breakfast an' lunch—sounds better'n 'binner', I guess.

We already had our meetin' clothes on an' Ellie wore that pretty pink dress her mama had brought over. Worse part was havin' to wear shoes again—plus doin' it all over when they have that Riley girl's funeral. We were gonna drop off Ellie at her folks so she could come with them.

"Let's take our tea an' go sit on the porch to eat our sandwiches…Ya'll want to?"

Ellie smiled an' pointed to Tiny.

Grandma smiled at her. "Of course, Ellie, but here, I have some scraps you can give her, too." She handed her a saucer with some ham trimmin's on it.

She smiled an' nodded.

"You're most welcome, honey."

We headed out the door an' down the hallway to the front porch. Tiny tagged along behind Ellie—she was still limpin' a bit.

Daddy was sittin' in a rocker when we got out there. He was just starin' out 'cross grandpa's pasture, sippin' on a Mason jar of sweet tea.

"What's the matter, Daddy?"

He turned an' looked at me. "Oh, just thinkin', Foot. Just thinking."

"'Bout what?"

He kinda pinched his lips together. "Thinking if there was anything else I could have done last night besides killing Mason Cobb."

"He was gonna shoot you, wasn't he?"

"Yeah, I expect he was."

"And he was gonna burn us all up, wadn't he?" added Hutch.

Daddy nodded. "I expect that's true, also."

"Didn't 'pear that there was a whole lot of choice, Daddy…Sure rather it'd be him than you."

He turned an' looked at all of us, one at a time. "Killing someone, kids…Taking their life forever, is not pleasant…No matter how bad they are, they're still human beings. Guess it's something I'll have to live with…Tom told me he remembers every man he had to kill up close in the war…still sees their faces…and they were the enemy."

Daddy took a sip of his tea an' studied the chunks of ice floatin' in the jar for a minute, then he looked up. "What's done is done."

"Would you do it again, Mister Joe?"

He looked at Hutch. "Guess I would, son…guess I would."

We all sat on the edge of the porch lettin' our legs hang off while we ate our sandwiches.

Ellie would take a bite an' hand Tiny one from the saucer grandma had give her. Think they like each other…an' Tiny don't take to just anybody.

Grandpa pulled up out front in the sheriff's car, got out an' walked up to the porch. Guess he'd been to town.

"Hi, Grandpa, better hurry if you want any of this brunch stuff. We near got it all."

"Oh, I'm sure your grandma will have somethin' for me. She and your mama cooking for after the service?"

"Yessir...Crowder peas an' cornbread an' I smelled a ham in the stove."

He shook his head an' smiled. "She's a wonder, she is."

Me an' Hutch looked at each other an' we both went, "Uh-Huh!"

Grandpa glanced at daddy before he grabbed the screen door handle. Think he could tell he was stewin' on somethin'.

"Joe, come on in the house for a minute, would you?"

Daddy got out of his rocker. "Sure, John. What do you need?"

"Need your advice on something." He held the door open for daddy to go on through.

Could hear 'em talking as they headed down the dog run toward the kitchen. Couldn't tell what they were sayin, but had a fair idea. Bet a quarter daddy will be in a better mood in just a little bit—think grandpa's a wonder, too.

JOLLEY'S CHAPEL CEMETERY

We dropped Ellie off at her mama an' daddy's house so she could go to the funerals with them. Doctor Duckworth had told grandpa to tell the Hargraves that she needed to be 'round people she knows—school chums an' the like.

Grandma tol' Miz Hargraves that Ellie's pink dress she had probably would be out of place at the funerals—I kinda liked it, though.

We went in both vehicles, like to church meetin', daddy's car an' the sheriff's car so we could carry the food again. Hutch got to come with us on account of it bein' a funeral an' not church.

Grandma an' mama carried the food to the same brush arbor we used for church that was right 'side the cemetery an' we could just walk over after the service.

Mister Tom had dug the two graves right close to each other so they put all those foldin' chairs in between. He was leanin' 'gainst a big loblolly pine over to the side of the cemetery watchin'—kinda outta the way. He'd fill the graves up after everbody left.

The preacher was leadin' everbody in singin' *Just a Closer Walk With Thee* while the rest of the folks was gettin' there.

Daddy an' mama sang along with it 'cause it was daddy's favorite hymn.

I am weak but Thou art strong

Jesus keep me from all wrong

I'll be satisfied as long

As I walk, let me walk close to Thee

Just a closer walk with Thee

Grant it, Jesus, is my plea

Daily walking close to Thee

Let it be, dear Lord, let it be

I like it, too.

Preacher Martin held his hand out for everbody to sit down an' he stood 'tween the two graves holdin' his Bible.

"Brothers an' sisters, I would like to read from Romans 6: verse 4:

'Therefore we are buried with him by baptism into death: that like as Christ was raised up from the dead by the glory of the Father, even so we also should walk in newness of life.'."

It was real quiet at the cemetery after the preacher read the passage from his Bible. But, it didn't last long. We all jumped at a real high scream from behind us back toward the road.

Everbody turned an' saw Ellie with her mama an' daddy at the entrance—one hand was to her mouth an' the other pointed our way. She screamed again…

§§§

EPILOGUE

JOLLEY'S CHAPEL CEMETERY

I turned to see what Ellie was pointin' at. Tom Rayford jerked forward from leaning against the pine tree, his right leg was folded up with his foot against the trunk. Think he thought she was pointin' his way—but she wadn't.

Ellie was screamin' over an' over again an' jumpin' up an' down an' cryin'.

Grandma got up an' went back to her, hurryin' fast as she could. Ellie's mama an' daddy were just standin' there lookin' kinda stunned an' didn't know what to do.

Grandma did. She grabbed aholt of Ellie an' hugged her tight.

Everbody else had got to their feet, too, not knowin' what was happenin' an' just watchin' Ellie who had stopped screamin' an' was sobbin' in grandma's arms.

Me an' Hutch didn't know what was happenin' either, but I saw Mister Tom out of the corner of my eye take off from his tree runnin'. I turned 'round an' he was chasin' the preacher who was runnin' fast as he could toward the woods like his hair was on fire.

Mister Tom tackled him 'fore he made it there. The preacher had dropped his Bible in the dirt at the graves, which I thought was kinda strange…'Course runnin' towards the woods while Ellie was screamin' an' cryin' was even stranger.

Daddy an' grandpa saw me an' Hutch turn around an' they did too.

Then the both of them took off toward Mister Tom an' the preacher who were 'rasslin' 'round on the ground over close to the woods. Preacher Martin was hittin' on Mister Tom, tryin' like the dickens to get up, but Mister Tom wadn't havin' any of it.

Grandpa reached down an' grabbed the preacher by his collar, jerked him to his feet, an' twisted one arm up behind his back.

"Ow, ow!" He woulda hollered calf-rope if he coulda thought of it.

"Now, what's goin' on, here?" He looked at Mister Tom.

"Ellie looked like she was pointing at the preacher, John, and he thought so too. He took off like a scalded dog." Mister Tom looked from grandpa to the preacher. "Dawned on me there was only one reason he would be runnin…"

Grandpa interrupted him an' nodded. "He's our killer and Ellie was pointin' him out." He looked down at Preacher Martin's brogans an' pointed. "Look, Joe, those match the prints I found at the first still…Showed 'em to you."

"Think you're right, John…Size is right, so's the heel."

The preacher squirmed in grandpa's grip, but gettin' loose from him would be like movin' a house.

"Let me go! How dare you! I'm a man of the cloth."

Grandpa's lip kinda curled up. "Yeah, dirty cloth."

He frog-hopped him back over to the graves.

Grandma had walked over to in front of the chairs where the preacher had been standin'. She still had an arm around Ellie's shoulders.

We could hear Ellie talkin' up a storm as we walked up. She looked up at grandma, an' then at grandpa.

"He's the one, Grandpa Jamison, he's the one. I watched him kill Bethany an' Loretta…Jennifer was with us, too."

Grandpa looked up at the rest of the congregation standin' close an' turned to daddy an' Mister Tom. "Get everybody back. They don't need to be hearin' all this…not goin' to court, they don't. Move 'em back."

Daddy an' Mister Tom walked shoulder to shoulder toward the others.

Daddy an' him held up their hands. "Ya'll get back, now, let John do his work. You'll find out all about this later. Now, please, move back."

Him an' Mister Tom walked forward with their hands held out in front of 'em forcin' everbody to move back where they couldn't hear what was goin' on.

"Go on, Ellie."

She looked at grandpa, there were tears in her eyes. "We had all been goin' to him reg'lar. Said we needed counselin'...that he was sent by God to purify us."

Grandma shook her head. "I think we know what that meant, honey. He was an evil, evil man."

She looked at grandma. "Yes, ma'am, figured that out, but we realized too late he was usin' us...We came to him an' told him we had all missed our time of the month...He said he had to baptize us for the final step to purification before we would be allowed into Heaven."

She choked back a sob an' took a deep breath. "We were down near a still somewhere near Three Creeks...He tied our hands, took Bethany's shoes off an' then walked her into the creek first, held her nose an' the back of her neck an' went to lean her back in the water…But he held her there with her face under an' she started strugglin' an' fightin'…" Ellie kinda bit her lip. "…he turned aloose of her nose an' grabbed the front of her throat still under the water. Bethany struggled some more…then she stopped."

She turned and buried her face in grandma's front.

"It's all right, honey, it's all right."

"She's lying. Can't you see she's lying?" There was kind of a look of panic on the preacher's face…Couldn't see nothin' but white around his eyes.

"The little twit is makin' it all up."

I didn't know what a twit was, but kinda figured it wadn't a nice thing to say.

Ellie looked him right in the face. "Then you shoved her away to float downstream like she was so much trash."

He turned to grandpa. "It's not true…You can't believe her…They were all just trollops."

There was another word I didn't know what was, but I bet it wadn't good neither.

"You took Loretta's shoes off too, an' was doin' the same thing." She turned to grandpa. "Me an' Jennifer started workin' on our ropes an' I got mine loose just in time to jump up an' run off into the woods as he shoved Loretta's body away to float off too."

"He got up on the bank an' chased after me…Yellin' for me to stop." Ellie started sobbin' again. "I ran an' ran until I couldn't run no more…I finally stopped, turned around an' couldn't hear nothin', guess he gave up when he couldn't catch me…but I was lost." Ellie looked at grandma, then grandpa. "Did Jennifer get away, too?"

Grandpa made a face an' shook his head.

Ellie turned to grandma again as grandpa twisted the preacher around and looked in his eye.

"Were there any more besides Bethany Cade, Loretta Harker, Jennifer Riley, and Ellie…Plus those two three weeks ago?"

He stared at the ground a minute.

Grandpa pushed his arm a little higher up his back. Thought his shoulder was gonna come outta the socket.

He leaned his head back like he was hurtin, an' I bettcha anything he was. "Ahh, no, no…That was all. I swear."

Grandpa gritted his teeth. "You mean yet, you little sorry son…of…"

"John L.! Not here."

He glanced kinda sheepishly at grandma. "Yessum."

Then he looked back at the preacher an' I couldn't see his lips even move, but could sure hear him plain as day even though he leaned real close to the man's ear.

"I want to be there when they put your sorry ass in that chair." He turned to daddy. "Joe, there's some handcuffs in the sheriff's car in the glove box. Would you get them for me, please?"

"Be a pleasure, John."

Daddy walked over to the sheriff's Ford, got the handcuffs an' came back over to us.

"Mind if I have the honor?"

"Be my guest."

He brought the preacher's arm down an' held both of them together behind his back. Think it was like havin' steel bands wrapped around you to have my grandpa hold your arms together.

Daddy snapped one side over the preacher's right wrist. an' then the other on his left. He squeezed 'em up till you couldn't hear 'em click no more.

The preacher hollered.

"Ow, that's too tight."

Daddy looked at grandpa. "Did you hear something, John?"

Grandpa grinned an' shook his head. "Can't say as I did."

Grandma touched grandpa on the shoulder. "John, we need to finish the services. Who can say something over these poor girls?"

"I will, Miz Mame."

She looked at Mister Tom.

"I did it mor'n once in the war." He reached down an' picked up the preacher's Bible still layin' on the ground. "Ya'll don't mind?"

Mister Tom stood between the graves, brushed the dirt off the Bible, an' opened it. Looked like he knew where he wanted to go on account he turned right to it.

"First Corinthians 15:50-57: *'Now this I say, brethren, that flesh and blood cannot inherit the kingdom of God; neither doth corruption inherit incorruption.*

Behold, I shew you a mystery; We shall not all sleep, but we shall all be changed,

In a moment, in the twinkling of an eye, at the last trump: for the trumpet shall sound, and the dead shall be raised incorruptible, and we shall be changed. For this corruptible must put on incorruption, and this mortal must put on immortality.

So when this corruptible shall have put on incorruption, and this mortal shall have put on immortality, then shall be brought to pass the saying that is written, Death is swallowed up in victory.

O death, where is thy sting? O grave, where is thy victory? The sting of death is sin; and the strength of sin is the law. But thanks be to God, which giveth us the victory through our Lord Jesus Christ.'."

He looked up from the Bible an' around to everbody, an' never turned the page. "And John 3: 16: *'For God so loved the world, that he gave his only begotten Son, that whosoever believeth in him should not perish, but have everlasting life.'*...Amen."

I think everbody there said 'Amen'."

We all loaded back up an' left Mister Tom to do what he had to do. Grandpa an' daddy went in the sheriff's car 'cause they were gonna take that killer preacher into town an' put him in the jailhouse.

TOM RAYFORD'S HOME

The next mornin', a hour or so after sunup, me, Hutch, an' Tiny were with grandpa as he pulled up in front of Mister Tom's cement house in his truck. Behind us was daddy in his car, an' he had grandma, mama, Bobby, Don, Hubert, an' Jessie.

We all got out an' I guess Mister Tom heard us drive up 'cause he come out the front door. "What's all this?" He pulled his overall strap over his shoulder, an' then hooked the other one, too.

Grandpa started passin' out baskets. "Happen to notice you had a bunch of fruit that needed pickin' before they started falling to the ground or the birds get half of 'em, Tom." He looked at the rest of us. "All right, let's get to it before it gets hot."

Everbody headed to the orchards. We had peaches, figs, an' plums to pick. Grandma had made a couple gallons of ice tea an' she set the metal water can she poured 'em in with the spigot on the bottom on the back of grandpa's truck.

She walked up to Mister Tom an' patted him on the chest. "Know how you like pickled peaches and fig preserves, Tom. I'll make up a bunch for you." Grandma winked at him an' headed toward the peach trees.

Grandpa was just standin' there watchin' everbody start pickin'. I was still close enough to hear what he was sayin' when he turned to Mister Tom.

"You, me, and the boys will haul what you want to sell into town to my regular route, tomorrow mornin', Tom." He grinned. "It won't last long…I would wager. Most of them know we're comin'."

Mister Tom didn't say nothin', but I could see a tear rollin' down his cheek…wadn't sure why. But I guess Medal of Honor war heroes don't talk a whole lot.

Me, daddy, Hutch, an' Tiny took off walkin' down 'tween two rows of peach trees.

"Let's start at the end, boys an' work back, what say?"

He put his arm around my shoulder as Hutch grabbed a peach from a tree next to him an' ate on it while we walked. "This'll be a summer you'll remember, won't it, Foot?"

I nodded, then looked up at him. "Did you an' grandpa have a talk 'bout killin' old man Cobb?"

He looked kinda surprised. "How'd you know about that?"

"Oh, just figured that's what he wanted to talk to you 'bout when you went in the house."

"You're pretty observant for a little fella."

I grinned. "I know."

"You know, Hossfly, sometimes a man has to do what a man has to do…and it's not always pleasant. But, your gut will tell you if it's the right thing to do or not…A good man always goes with his gut."

"Does that go for little boys, too?"

He nodded. "Goes for little boys, too."

I stopped an' daddy did too, then I reached up an' put my arms around his neck.

"I love you, Daddy."

He hugged me real tight an' I could feel him catch his breath.

"I love you, too, Foot…I love you, too."

THREE CREEKS

§§§§§

PREVIEW
THE NEXT EXCITING
NOVEL FROM

KEN FARMER

DALIA MARRH

Book #6
of the
SILKE JUSTICE SERIES

CHAPTER ONE

VALLES CALDERA

"I never knew the stars could look like that." *Dalia Marrh* walked backward, leading her snow white filly, Wind Runner and looking up at the expansive Milky Way that splashed across the night sky.

Silke and Haven Justice, along with Bone and Loraine, *Anompoli Lawa*, and Texas Ranger Riley

Boston also gazed skyward, happy to see the stars and be home as they walked toward the horses.

Bear Dog scooted ahead to his buddies, the horses left on this side of the portal, sniffing the familiar scents of home as he ran.

Dalia Marrh was the tall, slim daughter of Anasazi Shaman, *Enah Mahah*, Gentle Sky. She made it through the portal into the third world from the fourth of the Anasazi and the evil Skinwalkers before it was closed by *Anompoli Lawa*.

She had never seen the stars, moon, or the sun in her twenty-eight years—this was her first time in the third world.

The horses nickered at their approach. They had been without water and the grass in their picket area was nipped down to the dirt.

The strains of the William Tell Overture wafted around the group, seemingly coming from nowhere.

Wind Runner was the first to be startled, reared up, whinnied, and pawed the air. The other horses also reacted, bucking at the ends of their tethers and stomping their hooves at the strange sound.

Loraine turned. “Bone! That’s your phone’s ringtone.”

"Yeah, dang, who knew? Hadn't heard it in so long almost forgot." He fished it out of his possibles pouch, swiped the screen with his thumb and looked at the caller ID.

"Bone…Hey, what's shaking, Stella?" He turned to the others. "Lord love a duck, the vortex is fluxin' again."

BONE RANCH - 2020

"Damn you, Bone, we haven't heard from you for two months."

The 5'2" blonde bombshell Inspector with the Gainesville, Texas, Police Department glanced at her best friend, Police Forensics Technician, Peach Presley.

The pair were house and dog sitting for Bone and his godfather, Padrino, at their six hundred and forty acre ranch in Cooke County, Texas. The two, along with Loraine, had been transported from 2018 Texas to 1898 through a time travel type of portal.

They were in the root cellar with shelves on three sides loaded with put-by vegetables in Mason jars, jams, and preserves, along with fresh dug potatoes, onions, and apples in bushel baskets underneath the kitchen at the one hundred and twenty year old house on the Bone ranch that belonged to Sheriff Flynn's sister and her husband in the late 1890s and into the next century.

Stella and Peach were standing next to the Neolithic twenty inch tall solid gold statue with a three pound ruby mounted in the center that had been found on the ranch. The statue had been determined to be of the Paracas culture from between 100 and 800 BCE in Peru—predating the Inca.

Anompoli Lawa had postulated that the 7,000 carat ruby absorbed electromagnetic energy from cosmic rays and could activate a vortex that would connect to the past and Bone's cell phone if he was in an equal area of strong electromagnetic energy—per Einstein's theory of Special Relativity about the past, present, and future existing side-by-side at the same time in quantum entanglement.

"Put it on speaker, girl friend," said Peach, the Georgia native. "Hey, hidey Bone, how ya'll are?"

Bone's voice came through the speaker, "Hey, Peach, how you be, girl?"

"Bright eyed an' bushy tailed…Aw you know, mud an' magnolias, Bone…mud an' magnolias…Loraine there with yuh?"

"Yeah, couldn't prise us apart with a crowbar."

"Hey, Peach…Stella."

"Hey, Loraine," they answered simultaneously.

"Padrino, too?" asked Stella.

"No, he's back in Gainesville at Faye's…but *Anompoli Lawa's* with us. We're in New Mexico, near Santa Fe," replied Bone.

Stella and Peach exchanged glances and puzzled expressions.

"Thank God Winchester's with you to keep ya'll out of trouble an' make sure ya'll act like you got some sense…Now, what in God's green earth are ya'll in New Mexico for, Honey?"

"You wouldn't believe me if I told you, Peach."

"Bone, we already know you're three gallons of crazy in a two gallon bucket…If we can buy us talkin' over a hundred an' twenty years with a cell phone, we can buy most anythin' ya'll can get involved in."

"Well, you asked for it...We've been chasin' Skinwalkers and went through another kind of portal to their dimension known as the Fourth World where the missing Anasazi also are."

Stella and Peach looked at each other again, then down at Bone's dog, a blond and white pit bull named Tyrin—he cocked his head.

Stella took a breath. "You're right, Bone...that's a bit hard to swallow. Kinda like tryin' to eat some of Peach's baked possum and sweet potatoes."

Peach tugged at Stella's sleeve. "What the Sam Hill's a Skinwalker?"

"Ya'll remember those Caddo shape shifters that could change into giant wolves when we got involved with the Blue Water Woman?"

"Uh...yeah," they said together.

"Kinda the same thing...Except the Skinwalkers are evil demons, and damn hard to kill."

Stella leaned over to the phone. "I'm assumin' since we're talkin', ya'll got the job done."

"Could say. We killed a bunch of them and managed to close the 'always' portal to their world...lost a good friend, though."

"Anybody we know?"

"No, it was *Dalia Marrh's* father, *Enah Mahah*...Means Gentle Sky."

"Uh, who's *Dalia Marrh*, Bone?"

"She's an Anasazi maiden that came back through the portal with us. Her name means Pretty Moon." Bone turned to a once again wide-eyed *Dalia Marrh.* "Say hello to our friends, Stella and Peach…Just talk at this little box thing in my hand."

Bone held the phone facing her.

Dalia looked at the others, especially *Anompoli Lawa*, who nodded. She stared closely at the device, before leaning over. "Hello…I am *Dalia Marrh*. I am very pleased to meet you…I think."

Stella and Peach smiled and raised their eyebrows.

Peach pulled Stella's hand with the phone closer. "I gotta say, sweetheart, that your name's pretter than a speckled horse in a daisy pasture…*Dalia Marrh*…Just love it to death an' back."

Dalia Marrh glanced at Loraine who smiled. "Means they like your name…Think it's very pretty."

Dalia leaned forward again. "Thank you."

"You're just welcome as buttermilk pie, Honey."

Static started to build in Bone's phone. "Looks like we're losing connection and breaking up, kids. Try again soon…Laterbye."

"Laterbye, ya'll. It…" Peach's voice cut off before she could finish.

Dalia turned to *Anompoli Lawa.* "I don't understand."

He smiled. "Well, I won't say it's simple, child, but it's very similar to the portal we just came through back in the cave except it was smaller and we were only talking through it to the future and them us. The portals can do several things, including going back and forth in time, besides going to other dimensions."

She blinked her big brown eyes several times, paused, and then looked at the venerable Shaman and nodded. "I see."

Bone smiled and looked at Loraine. "Well, that was nice…Betcha they do what they did with *Te*

Ata after Silke met her at her induction into the Hatchet Woman Clan…and do a bunch of research on the internet."

Anompoli Lawa nodded and looked at *Dalia Marrh*. "*Te Ata*, Chickasaw meaning, Bearer of the Dawn…Also a beautiful name. She became a great storyteller and spokesperson for the Chickasaw."

Dalia pursed her perfectly formed lips and nodded. "It is a beautiful name."

"Well, folks, let's get those horses down to the water before they get really mad…Ranger, we'll take care of doing that and picketing them on some fresh graze if you'll gather some deadfall and blowdown for the fire. Don't know about ya'll but I could use some supper."

The Ranger nodded at Bone and headed into the woods.

An hour later, the horses had all been watered and picketed on fresh graze. Everyone sat around finishing their supper of beans and bacon with cups of hot coffee. They all seemed to be gazing up at the stars that looked like millions and millions of twinkling campfires.

Silke glanced at *Dalia*. “Lot different than just starin’ at pitch black isn’t it, Pretty Moon?”

She nodded. “It is, it is indeed.”

Haven took a sip of her coffee and turned to the Anasazi. “I’ve been wonderin’ *Dalia*, how is it you speak so correctly, I mean you livin’ in the other world an’ all.”

She smiled. “My father, *Enah Mahah*, brought a number of books…what he called your classics through. He taught me to read, write, and speak your language when I was young. I read them all, numerous times…Plutarch, Herodotus, Sophocles, Plato, Euripides, Homer, Shakespeare, and your Bible.”

Anompoli Lawa shook his head in wonder. “He was one of the most brilliant men I’ve ever had the pleasure to meet and know…He was a great doctor, too.”

“I have often wondered what it would be like to study medicine, go back and help my people.”

Bone reached forward with his glove, grabbed the pot, and refilled his cup. “Could happen, *Dalia Marrh*, could happen.”

Silke looked off in the dark back toward the cave. “Could be some time before you can go back though, *Dalia.* We would have to find either another 'always' portal or an open 'sometimes' one."

"Know what goes with those, don't you, Cuz?"

Silke paused a moment. "I do, Haven…I certainly do."

§§§

OTHER NOVELS FROM
TIMBER CREEK PRESS

www.timbercreekpress.net

MILITARY ACTION/TECHNO

BLACK EAGLE FORCE: Eye of the Storm (Book #1)
by Buck Stienke and Ken Farmer

BLACK EAGLE FORCE: Sacred Mountain (Book #2) by Buck Stienke and Ken Farmer

RETURN of the STARFIGHTER (Book #3)
by Buck Stienke and Ken Farmer

BLACK EAGLE FORCE: BLOOD IVORY (Book #4)
by Buck Stienke and Ken Farmer with Doran Ingrham

BLACK EAGLE FORCE: FOURTH REICH (Book #5) by Buck Stienke and Ken Farmer

AURORA: INVASION (Book #6 in the BEF) by Ken Farmer & Buck Stienke

BLACK EAGLE FORCE: ISIS (Book #7) by Buck Stienke and Ken Farmer

BLOOD BROTHERS - Doran Ingrham, Buck Stienke and Ken Farmer

DARK SECRET - Doran Ingrham

NICARAGUAN HELL - Doran Ingrham

BLACKSTAR BOMBER by T.C. Miller

BLACKSTAR BAY by T.C. Miller

BLACKSTAR MOUNTAIN by T.C. Miller
BLACKSTAR ENIGMA by T.C. Miller

HISTORICAL FICTION WESTERN
THE NATIONS by Ken Farmer and Buck Stienke
HAUNTED FALLS by Ken Farmer and Buck Stienke
HELL HOLE by Ken Farmer
ACROSS the RED by Ken Farmer and Buck Stienke
BASS and the LADY by Ken Farmer and Buck Stienke
DEVIL'S CANYON by Buck Stienke
LADY LAW by Ken Farmer
BLUE WATER WOMAN by Ken Farmer
FLYNN by Ken Farmer
AURALI RED by Ken Farmer
COLDIRON by Ken Farmer
STEELDUST by Ken Farmer
BONE by Ken Farmer
BONE'S LAW by Ken Farmer
BONE & LORAINE by Ken Farmer
BONE'S GOLD by Ken Farmer
BONE'S ENIGMA by Ken Farmer
SILKE JUSTICE by Ken Farmer
SILKE'S QUEST by Ken Farmer
NO TIME to DIE by Buck Stienke

SILKE'S RIDE by Ken Farmer
ANGEL JUSTICE by Ken Farmer
SKINWALKER JUSTICE by Ken Farmer

SY/FY

LEGEND of AURORA by Ken Farmer & Buck Stienke
AURORA: INVASION (Book #6 in the BEF) by Ken Farmer & Buck Stienke

HISTORICAL FICTION ROMANCE

THE TEMPLAR TRILOGY

MYSTERIOUS TEMPLAR by Adriana Girolami
THE CRIMSON AMULET by Adriana Girolami
TEMPLAR'S REDEMPTION by Adriana Girolami

MYSTERY

BONE'S PARADOX by Buck Stienke
THE LOCK BOX by Terry D. Heflin
THREE CREEKS by Ken Farmer
THREE CREEKS by Ken Farmer
RED HILL ROAD by Ken Farmer
THE POND by Ken Farmer
UNION COUNTY by Ken Farmer
KILGORE by Ken Farmer

CIVIL WAR ROMANACE
SCARLET HEM by Terry D. Heflin

Coming Soon

HISTORICAL FICTION WESTERN
McGRATH by T.C. Miller
DALIA MARRH by Ken Farmer

CIVIL WAR ROMANCE
GOLDEN CIRCLE by Terry D. Heflin

HISTORICAL FICTION ROMANCE
DAUGHTER of HADES by Adriana Girolami
ZAMINDAR and the LADY by Adriana Girolami

SY/FY
ANTAREAN DILEMMA by T.C. Miller

MYSTERY
RECIPE for MURDER by Ken Farmer & Buck Stienke
SIN NO MORE by Ken Farmer & Buck Stienke
OLD DOGS an' OLD ROADS by Ken Farmer

Thanks for reading *THREE CREEKS.* If you enjoyed it, I would really appreciate a review on Amazon.

You may contact me at pagact@yahoo.com
My FaceBook Page:
www.facebook.com/KenFarmerAuthor/
Amazon Author Page:
www.amazon.com/Ken-Farmer/e/B0057OT3YI

TIMBER CREEK PRESS

Made in the USA
Monee, IL
09 February 2022